A BEAUFONT SHORT STORIES COLLECTION

A BEAUFONT SHORT STORIES COLLECTION

SARAH NOFFKE

MICHAEL ANDERLE

THE MYSTERIOUS PLATO

A BEAUFONT SHORT STORY BOOK 1

CHAPTER ONE

The destruction littered all around the hotel didn't affect the happy mood in the space. In the lobby bar, laughter rose over the festive piano music. Hotel guests were talking excitedly about the events that had occurred.

Many of them glanced at the unlikely trio in the corner—curious about the strange animals who'd congregated around a table and were drinking a bottle of whiskey. However, the owners of Hotel Laguna Maldita had said the magical animals could stay because they'd brought good luck to the small coastal tourist destination. No one knew that they were responsible for saving it.

The large wrought iron chandelier that hung in the middle of the lobby was still intact, but recent events had knocked out many of its candles. Cracks in the plaster and broken paintings on the wall were reminders of the battle waged inside Hotel Laguna Maldita. The broken floor-to-ceiling windows that showed views of the now placid lagoon were shattered reminders of the fracas that had happened outside the hotel. Coconuts and debris were strewn across the lawn—all signs of the storm that had passed.

"That was a close one," Faraday, the talking squirrel said from his perch on the table—his fluffy tail flicking in the humid Mexico air.

"I know." Lunis, the large blue dragon sidled up to the table, but most of his body and tail were on the floor or trailing out onto the patio area of the large hotel lobby. "I didn't know if we'd pull it all off in time."

"The way it all worked out was crazy," Faraday mused, stirring his drink with a cocktail straw before sipping.

"I know." Lunis turned to look at the inconspicuous black and white cat sitting with them at the table in the corner. "It's like someone masterminded it all and put us in the right place at the right time, leaving clues as to how we were to handle the strange events."

"Yes, like we were the pawns, playing against the king," Faraday seethed, turning his large brown eyes on the magical lynx on the other side of the table.

"I wasn't using you as pawns," Plato, the cat said dryly, seemingly bored. "Nor were you playing against a king on the board."

"Yeah, well, where were you the entire time?" Steam issued from Lunis' mouth as the waiter brought another bottle of whiskey. He left it on the table when Plato nodded consent to him and retreated without a word.

"Yeah, we know you were there the entire time, orchestrating things from the shadows. Like you do," Faraday added.

"I was having a bad hair day so I decided to work remotely." Plato watched as the dragon poured them all another round of drinks.

"You were setting all this up so we'd fight the king on the chessboard you'd arranged," Lunis countered.

Plato blinked at the large blue dragon. "If we're quite honest, the king wasn't even on the board yet."

"What does that mean?" Faraday's nose twitched.

"I think I know." Lunis looked over his shoulder as the music in the main area picked up and the hotel guests got louder.

"I think you do." Plato looked around the hotel lobby bar.

Lunis turned back. "First, I want you to tell us what happened. I know where I was when everything went down. I think I know where Faraday was for the most part, although I'd appreciate a rundown. However, I want to know what you've been up to, Plato."

The magical lynx who'd been around since the dawn of time nodded. "Okay, fine. I'll tell you. All of these events started around three days ago…"

CHAPTER TWO

Three Days Previously...

"Will you pass the sunscreen?" Liv Beaufont asked from under her large floppy hat. Her oversized sunglasses made her look like a movie star in hiding. She was, as it were... hiding, but not a movie star.

Unhurried, Plato, the black and white American short-haired cat pulled his gaze from the emerald-blue ocean and smirked at her. "I can't."

"Is it because I didn't say 'please' again?" Annoyance sprang to Liv's face.

"No, it's because I don't have hands."

Even behind her large shades, Plato knew that the Warrior for the House of Fourteen had rolled her eyes. With a groan, she got up and retrieved the beach bag on the other side of Plato's lounge chair.

The pair had the perfect spot on the beach in Tortugas Locas —a popular tourist destination in the south of Mexico. Thankfully, Liv's money had gotten them the entire resort all to themselves. Her reputation working for Father Time didn't hurt either. Liv and Plato were overdue for a vacation after quite literally saving the planet—yet again.

Now Liv and Plato could hide out from would-be enemies and relax for a bit. The only things missing were the other Beaufonts and Stefan, Liv's husband. However, since they all had important missions going on, they couldn't get away simultaneously.

Liv plopped back down in her lounge chair and began smearing sunblock on her arms and legs. She glanced around the empty resort, the infinity pool behind them giving off a reflection that made her squint. "You'd think since I bought out the entire place that I'd have incredible service."

"You scare them," Plato stated matter-of-factly.

Liv grinned slyly. "Because I carry a sword to dinner?"

"That's partly why."

Liv pushed up to a standing position again, pulling a cover-up from the beach bag. "Well, even if I'm on vacation, it doesn't mean I can let down my guard. On my last vacation, pirates attacked the resort. They stormed in and ransacked the place and made all these unreasonable demands."

Plato shook his head. "Those were tourists from the north."

Liv shivered. "Their skin was so white that it burned my eyes. And seriously, socks with sandals. It was all too much."

"I think if you want a drink, you're going to have to get it yourself," Plato offered, his eyes scanning the waters ahead of them, picking up on a ship in the distance.

"I realize that." Liv secured her cover-up around her bikini. "Do you want anything?"

"World peace," he answered.

"Does that come with one olive or two?" Liv deadpanned.

"It comes with a miracle, I believe."

"I'll get you a whiskey instead." Liv strode for the resort's bar.

"Make it neat," Plato called to her retreating back.

He narrowed his eyes at the ship that cut through the whitecapped waters far in the distance. He believed he knew who was on board the vessel. More importantly, he was almost positive he knew what they came to Tortugas Locas to do. It was even more critical that he sprang into action and stopped them as soon as possible.

He glanced at the cell phone sitting on the table between the chairs and tapped it twice with his paw. A moment later, it *dinged* with a text message from one of the most important entities on the planet.

Plato knew that Liv deserved a vacation, but she wouldn't get it if she hung around this place. No, Plato and a few of his friends could handle the events about to unfold. Liv didn't need to be involved. Thankfully, Father Time knew that—he'd summoned her to his side.

Liv returned a moment later with a colorful slushy drink that was undoubtedly mostly full of vodka and a whiskey served neat.

"I wouldn't take a sip of that yet." Plato waited until she'd settled down and sighed before bringing the straw to her lips.

She paused and arched an eyebrow behind her oversized sunglasses. "Why is that?"

"Because you got a message from Papa Creola." He used the name that only those who personally knew Father Time called him.

She sighed again, lowered the perspiring glass, and picked up her phone with her other hand. A moment later Liv grunted in frustration, giving Plato a look of annoyance. "Papa says—"

"That he needs you immediately," Plato interrupted.

"Yes, and that—"

"He has a top-secret case that requires Bellator, so bring your sword," Plato cut in again.

"Like I ever go anywhere without it," Liv muttered, putting down her drink. "He also said—"

"Not to have even a sip of that drink because you'll need your wits about you for the case, and you asked the bartender to go heavy on the vodka," Plato interrupted again.

Liv shook her head. "I'm not sure whether I should be more annoyed that Papa Creola knows what I order at a resort bar when he's thousands of miles away or that you know the contents of his text messages, which were unread."

Plato shrugged. "Or you could be impressed."

Gathering her bag and phone, Liv got up from the lounge chair. "Well, let's go see what that man wants. I should've known this whole vacation thing wasn't going to last. Maybe I shouldn't have told Papa Creola what I was doing."

"It's not like it would've mattered." Plato watched as the ship in the distance came closer to shore.

"Yes, you and he are all-knowing and full of mystery on how." Liv waved for Plato to get up. "Come on. We've got to go."

He shook his head, leaned over, and sipped his drink. "I'm staying."

Liv's mouth popped open. "I'm not allowed to drink and relax, but you get to?"

"I believe Papa's message asked for your immediate assistance, not mine."

She continued to gawk at him. "So you're going to stay here and lounge beachside while I go and save the world? That doesn't seem fair."

Plato sipped again, his eyes on the boat. "I'll send you a postcard."

Liv blew out a breath and pulled off her floppy hat to show a head of messy, long, blonde hair. Following his line of sight, she glanced over her shoulder at the boat and back to him. "Something tells me that you're not going to be taking cat naps and getting drunk."

"I don't nap," he said plainly.

"All right, you mysterious lynx." Liv opened a portal to Roya Lane, where Papa Creola would be waiting for her. "You stay and pretend not to be orchestrating some plan to save…well, whatever you're saving."

"Okay, and good luck with fixing the time-lapse." He didn't take his gaze off the boat.

"Time-lapse? How do you…is that what…never mind. I'll go and find out from Papa what I'm doing."

"I'm not at liberty to tell you more, anyway," Plato sang, lifting his paw and beginning to lick it casually.

"Not that you would. You and Papa love knowing what's going to happen but not overly sharing the details with the rest of us. You sneaky little masterminds."

She waved as she stepped through the portal and disappeared a moment later.

Plato let out a breath of relief, grateful that Liv was out of the way. It wasn't that she couldn't handle the events that would unravel in Tortugas Locas. It wasn't her job. If Plato was going to mastermind the very best solution, he'd rely on magical creatures rather than magicians.

CHAPTER THREE

The ship Plato had been watching anchored in the harbor ten minutes later. The three men on board had broken into an abandoned warehouse nearby. Now they hunched over a makeshift table.

The dim lantern light made it hard for the men to make out the map details they'd spread out in front of them. From the overhead rafters, Plato could see everything perfectly—his enhanced senses always operating.

"With the ocean on one side and the lagoon on the other, finding a stronghold in the city will be a challenge," Donte, the leader of the goons mused, tracing his fat finger down the strip of land on the map. He'd combed his black hair over one ear, attempting to cover the many scars on that side of his head. He wore a dirty leather jacket despite the humid temperatures.

"I don't understand what's so special about Tortugas Locas." Fishy Paul shook his head. "Why does the boss want us to take over this tourist trap of a city?"

"Because he does," Donte spat, narrowing his eyes at the other man. "You don't ask questions. You do as told."

Gruesome Kevin laughed. "Yeah, if you did, you wouldn't have fallen in that vat of fish guts, Fishy Paul." He waved in front of his nose, grimacing. "I swear you still stink a week later."

"Well, at least that smell will wear off," Fishy Paul spat. "Your face will never get better looking nor will you ever grow, Gruesome Kevin."

The other man was indeed shorter than average at barely over five-foot-six. If that wasn't enough to tease him about, he also had a large nose, a boxy chin, and beady little eyes, making him quite unattractive.

"Will you two knuckleheads shut your mouths?" Donte demanded, pressing his hand to his forehead. "I'm trying to think. We've got to find a way to run this city but it being a tourist destination makes it tough. There will always be new faces and a fluctuation in people."

"Yeah, unlike the last city we ran, there's no consistency here," Fishy Paul stated. The firelight illuminated the pockmarks on his face and his slicked-back gray hair. "Tortugas Locas' industry is all tourism."

Donte stood, drumming his fat fingers on the table. "Well, then that's what we'll run. We'll take over the tourism bureau. From there we can keep tabs on the hotels, transportation, food, and excursions. All of it will be our domain."

Gruesome Kevin cackled deeply. "That's genius. The whole city will answer to us in no time. They won't so much as change the lunch specials on menus without asking our permission."

Donte held up his hand like he was going to slap the other man. Gruesome Kevin flinched and took a step backward.

"It's not about control," Donte commanded. "Well, it is, but running a city is about skimming profits. The boss is smart because although getting dominance over this place will be a different challenge, the revenue potentials are astronomical."

"Yeah, the boss is pretty smart," Fishy Paul agreed. "You think we're ever going to meet him?"

Donte shook his head. "I haven't even met him. He gives me

my orders over the phone. Who cares? The point is that we get paid, especially after you mucked up the last job by falling into that vat of fish guts. No more mistakes, you hear?"

Fishy Paul held up his hands in surrender and nodded. "You got it, Donte."

Gruesome Kevin glanced around the damp and dark warehouse. "So is this our home base? I don't know how intimidating we're going to look surrounded by rotting crates and whatever else is in the shadows of this place."

"Yeah, this place sure isn't going to work." Donte returned his attention to the map. "We need a place with defenses. Not something on the main strip because it will be harder to watch our backs. And yeah, something that's fancy yet authentic. The boss was clear about that. The locals will respect us a lot more if we blend in."

"So not the Marriott, then?" Fishy Paul laughed.

Anger flashed on Donte's face, and he looked ready to assault the other man.

Seizing his chance, Plato conjured a single piece of paper in the air. It hovered in front of him for a moment before drifting to the table below him, landing on the map.

The three men, all spooked, pulled their guns and aimed at the flier that lay before them.

"What the—" Donte squinted at the piece of paper.

"Hey!" Gruesome Kevin yelled, looking up at the rafters, but he would only see darkness.

Fishy Paul fired, making a loud *popping* sound. The bullet tore through the paper and the barrel they'd been using as a makeshift table.

"You idiot!" Donte holstered his gun. "It's a stupid piece of paper. Why did you shoot it? You're going to bring attention to us."

"Sorry, Donte." Fishy Paul slid his free hand through his silver hair. The one holding the gun shook. "I'm tense after the last job."

Gruesome Kevin was still searching the rafters. "Where'd that paper come from?"

"Who cares?" Donte picked up the flier, the bullet hole from the gunfire having made a hole in the center. However, the main advertisement was still visible. He read the print on the top. "Hotel Laguna Maldita, now open under new ownership. Experience the magic of this secluded paradise on the lagoon. This small family-run boutique hotel offers all the amenities of the large resorts without the crowds and commotion."

Donte lowered the flier, his eyes wide. "This place sounds perfect." He checked the map, finding Hotel Laguna Maldita. "It's secluded and in a protected cove on the lagoon."

"Which means we won't be vulnerable to attacks." Fishy Paul holstered his gun, still shaking.

"My thoughts exactly," Donte agreed.

"It sounds authentic," Gruesome Kevin added. "I don't even know how to say its name."

"Hotel Laguna Maldita," Donte said. "It means cursed lagoon."

"Do you think that's safe?" Fishy Paul asked.

"Of course it is." Donte rolled up the map. "It's probably some superstition the locals have. In no time, the only thing they'll fear is us."

He strode for the door they came through. "Come on, you buffoons. We have work to do."

The other two men followed Donte out, leaving Plato alone in the rafters. His whiskers twitched with anticipation. So far everything was falling into place, but there were many more pieces to get onto the chessboard before the game could start.

CHAPTER FOUR

Plato wasn't as grateful for his enhanced senses when he magically appeared in the junkyard on the outskirts of Tortugas Locas. The smells of rust and decay competed for dominance among the heaps of broken-down equipment and trash.

From his spot sitting in the back of an old bus, Plato viewed the woman trudging around the junkyard. He knew her name was Doctor Beth Hailey. The mysterious lynx also knew what she was up to. He would've despite her talking to herself, telling her mission for anyone to hear.

The mad scientist thought she was alone. Other than Plato hiding in the broken-down bus, she was. However, Dr. Hailey spoke to herself no matter if she were alone or not—which was off-putting to most who witnessed it.

"Create a hurricane machine," she muttered while rummaging through various pieces of equipment in a tall pile. "What does the boss want with a hurricane machine?"

She pushed aside the hood of an old tractor, finding half of a dishwasher and a couple of bald tires. "What do I care, as long as he pays up."

Not having found what she was looking for, the magician

turned, searching the vast area. "What I need is an old boiler. Add some magitech and the equipment I already have, and voilà, it should make a hurricane."

She shook her head of loose red hair that fell past her shoulders. "Again, why that man wants to make hurricanes is beyond me. Thankfully, storms don't scare me. Why fear natural disasters when I have science on my side to protect me?"

Dr. Hailey picked up her long skirt and strode down the path that snaked between the piles of junk. "Where is the old boiler section? Why can't someone organize all this stuff? That would make my job easier."

Her eyes lit up when she spotted a set of old water heaters together in a loose pile. A moment later, all the excitement disappeared from her face. "These are all too new. When they say they don't make them like they used to, it's the truth. The new stuff wears out. They built the old equipment to last. That's what I need for a hurricane machine."

It was Plato's turn to lead Dr. Beth Hailey onto his unseen chessboard. The magical lynx conjured a tourist brochure for Tortugas Locas. It drifted down from the open window of the bus where he sat and landed at Dr. Hailey's feet.

She *harrumphed* at the pamphlet in her path and stuck her hands on her hips, looking down at it as though it was blocking her progress. "Can't you see I'm looking for something?"

Plato blinked twice, and a sudden breeze swept through the air, making Dr. Hailey's hair move in the wind and flip through the pages of the tourist brochure. It stopped on a large full-page advertisement.

Dr. Hailey was about to move around the magazine when something on the page caught her eyes. "Wait!" she exclaimed, reaching down and picking up the brochure, her gaze hurriedly running over the advertisement. "Hotel Laguna Maldita—built a hundred years ago. Old World charm with modern conveniences.

Enjoy this magical oasis on the lagoon. Family owned and operated."

She lowered the brochure with a triumphant look. "A building from the turn of the last century would have the type of boiler parts I need. The lagoon is the perfect place to build and test the hurricane machine. Looks like I'll have my money in no time."

Pivoting at once, Dr. Hailey made her way to the junkyard's exit, the tourist brochure with the address to Hotel Laguna Maldita clutched in her hands.

Plato smiled. Now that he'd set up one side of the chessboard, it was time to arrange the other half. That's where his magical friends came into play—although they'd have no idea they'd be playing this game until after it started.

CHAPTER FIVE

From the shadows of the grand piano that sat in the lobby of Hotel Laguna Maldita, Plato had a perfect place to watch the events that would unravel next. He was camouflaged by the black and white piano, matching it perfectly.

"Do you hear that incessant racket?" Francesca Ward asked, her Spanish accent thick. She had her hands on her hips as she regarded the wall before her in the lobby of Hotel Laguna Maldita. A loud pounding like that of a heartbeat echoed from the stucco walls.

"It's old pipes, dear," her husband Jack Ward explained. "It's an old building, and they always have strange noises."

"Weird noises is one thing." Francesca pursed her lips at her husband. "It's not only that. My things keep going missing. There are freezing spots throughout the hotel when the air conditioner isn't running. And I swear I saw someone walking down the hallway last night."

Jack gave his daughter, Laura, a cautious look. She was stationed beside them in the lobby at a table doing her math homework. She looked up now, curiosity in her large brown eyes. The twelve-year-old had her father's light-colored hair but her mother's Hispanic features, like her mocha eyes and olive skin.

Francesca had been born and raised in San Miguel de Allende but had moved to the United States for college. That's where they'd had Laura, but seeking a new adventure, the family had bought Hotel Laguna Maldita. The price had been nearly a steal, and none of the locals seemed at all interested in the old hotel—giving them strange looks when the family mentioned they'd be running it.

Booking guests had already proven to be a challenge, which was why Jack had started advertising in local tourist brochures and posting fliers. He was in charge of marketing and running the front desk. Francesca was the chef and bartender.

As for Laura, well, they expected her to keep up with her studies if she wanted to practice soccer in her free time. The little girl hadn't liked moving away from her friends and school in the United States, but her parents were hopeful that in time, she'd appreciate growing up in a place that people flocked to for vacations.

"I'm sure you saw a guest out of their room late," Jack told his wife, returning his attention to her.

Francesca shook her head. The bun holding her dark brown hair tied up swayed from the movement. "We hardly have any guests, and the ones we do weren't on the third floor where I saw someone."

"You've been working hard on new recipes for the restaurant, dear," Jack consoled. "I'm sure you're exhausted."

The walls thundered like something was inside them and trying to get out. Francesca jumped. Jack tensed. Laura laughed, seemingly amused.

Wringing her hands together, Francesca shook her head again. "No, it's this place. I can't rest properly, and it's always got me on edge."

Jack laid a consoling hand on his wife's shoulder. "We're new to this. The hotel is old. We're going to work out the kinks. Then this place will thrive, and we'll have the dream of hospitality like we always wanted."

Francesca opened her mouth to argue, but three men strode through the arched entryway into the hotel.

Catching sight of them, Jack gave his wife an excited look, hoping that they were about to check in new customers. "Laura, why don't you help your mother in the kitchen with preparations for dinner service."

"But—"

"Now," her father urged.

Laura nodded and followed her mother into the kitchen at the back as Jack turned to greet the three mobsters—who he mistook as paying customers.

CHAPTER SIX

"Hello, gentlemen." Jack Ward smiled at the three men, who all had wide shoulders and wore jackets, although it was a usually hot day in Tortugas Locas. "What can I do for you?"

The man in the front, who had black hair parted on one side and awkwardly combed over the side of his head, looked around the lobby. "Yeah, I like this place. I think this could do just fine."

"Are you looking for accommodations?" Jack was probably thinking that renting three rooms would help out greatly since the hotel only had twenty. Every little bit would help to cover costs and get the business off the ground.

"We are," the guy said. "More importantly, we're looking for a place to conduct business."

"Oh," Jack said with surprise. "What kind of business are you into?"

"I'm Donte." He indicated the men behind him. "These are my associates, Paul and Kevin. We're in the business of managing things."

"M-M-Managing things." Jack scratched his head of light-colored hair, obviously not following.

"Yeah, we're new to town." Fishy Paul looked up at the

wrought iron chandelier hanging from the vaulted ceiling. "We're the kind of guys you want to know. We're going to make a name for ourselves here in Tortugas Locas. Managing things, if you know what I mean."

"I-I-I don't think I do," Jack admitted.

Donte shot Fishy Paul a look of annoyance. "I think what my associate means to say is that we have plans of doing business here in Tortugas Locas, and we think your hotel could make a perfect home base for our meetings. What do you say, mister…"

"Ward. Jack Ward."

Donte smiled and nodded. "So what do you say? Can we get a few rooms and use your lobby and grounds for our meetings?"

"Well…yes, on the rooms." Jack strode behind the front desk beside them. "I'm not sure about having meetings here. This is supposed to be a relaxing place for families to unwind."

"Jack, I think you'll find that having us around will be good for business," Donte stated. "We tend to have a way of encouraging people to stay, and I dare say by the looks of things, you could use more guests."

"Well, that's true." Jack flipped open the reservation book.

"Having us around is like a lucky charm," Gruesome Kevin imparted. "We can protect you—if you know what I mean."

"Again, I don't," Jack admitted.

Donte put his hands on the front desk and leaned forward. "There can be some sketchy types in these parts. You'd be wise to align yourself with people who know how to navigate things. Who can ensure your business does well and others business, well, doesn't do so well. You get my drift?"

Jack blinked, his heart suddenly beating fast in his chest.

"Tell you what." Donte leaned back. "Why don't you let us set up shop here, and we'll try it out on a probationary basis?"

"Well, I guess that couldn't hurt," Jack admitted, his face screwed up with indecision.

"Of course it can't." Donte smiled.

Something banged against the closest wall, making the whole lobby vibrate like there was an earthquake. All three men pulled guns from beneath their jackets—pointing them at the offending wall.

Jack's arms shot up into the air, his eyes wide. "Whoa! Whoa! That's nothing."

"Doesn't sound like nothing," Donte said, his gun still pointed at the wall.

"It's only old pipes," Jack explained, his voice shaking. "This place is old, and the boiler is on the fritz, I think."

"Yeah, I guess that makes sense." Donte nodded at the other two men, and they all holstered their guns. He glanced at a visibly rattled Jack. "So those rooms. How about 'em?"

Jack cleared his throat, checking the reservation book. "Yes, of course. The nightly rate for a standard room is—"

"I think we're misunderstanding," Donte interrupted. "As I mentioned, we're the kind of guys you want to have around. Think of us like security. But we're more than that. Those who we like, prosper. Those we don't, end up in a bad place."

"Are you saying you're not paying for the rooms?" Jack blinked at Donte with confusion and fear.

Gruesome Kevin looked around the lobby. "This sure is a nice place. I'd hate it if there was a fire and it burned to the ground."

"That's true," Fishy Paul added. "I bet you have to clean the gutters sometimes. It would be too bad if you fell off the ladder doing maintenance and broke a leg or two."

Donte smiled, his gaze on Jack. "You see, with us around, it's like insurance. I can assure you that bad things won't happen to you if we're around. However, if we're not, if we can't stay here, well, then bad things could happen to you and your hotel. See?"

Supremely flustered, Jack frantically flipped through the reservation book. "I think we have some rooms you three would like on the third floor. I'll retrieve the keys for you right now."

He turned for the wall of room keys behind him and quickly grabbed three of them at once.

"Good." Donte smiled wickedly. "I'm glad that we could reach an agreement. Look, we're already bringing you good fortune. I see another customer has arrived."

Jack turned, holding up the keys as a woman with red hair and a crazed look in her eyes waltzed into the lobby of Hotel Laguna Maldita.

CHAPTER SEVEN

Donte swiped the keys from Jack's shaking hand with a victorious smile and strode off for the stairs. The other two marched after him with cocky looks on their ugly faces.

Dr. Beth Hailey waved her hand in front of her face, shaking her head. "One of those guys, or all of them smell."

"Maybe they've been on a fishing excursion." Jack pressed his hands down on the front desk, trying to quell his nervousness. "How may I help you?"

"I'm looking for a room for the next few days." Dr. Hailey looked around the hotel.

"Of course." Jack flipped through the reservation book, although over half the rooms were unoccupied. "The nightly rate is one hundred and eighty-nine dollars."

"That's fine." Dr. Hailey glanced at the open doors on the other side of the lobby, where the bar and restaurant were, followed by the patio and lawn area. "The gazebo area out there would be ideal for my experiments."

"What you'd say?" Jack looked up from the reservation book.

Dr. Hailey turned back. "Nothing. I wasn't talking to you."

"Right." Jack drew out the word. "We have a room on the—"

The noise in the wall sounded more like knocking and hissing this time. Jack sighed. "Sorry, that's the boiler and pipes. I'm calling someone to take a look at them. I'll put you on the third floor where you won't be disturbed."

"Boiler," Dr. Hailey said at once, excitedly. "It won't bother me. The boiler is on the first floor. I'll take a room on the main level."

"Oh, well, I didn't want you to be disturbed. Especially if they have to do repairs."

"I'm a scientist. Doctor Beth Hailey at your service." She bowed slightly. "Why don't I take a look at the boiler for you? I might be able to help with it."

"Oh, what kind of a scientist?"

"A technical one." Dr. Hailey appeared to be hunting for the right words. The truth was that she was a magitech scientist but didn't want anyone to know that.

"Well, I suppose if you wouldn't mind," Jack stated. "It's much appreciated."

"Not a problem." Dr. Hailey strode over to the wall where the knocking was still echoing. "Yes, it's an old boiler, exactly like what I need…"

"Did you say need?" Jack asked. "You need an old boiler?"

Dr. Hailey straightened. "I need to study an old boiler. This will be perfect, and I can fix yours."

"Oh, well, that does seem like a good arrangement." Jack turned around and retrieved a key. He handed it to Dr. Hailey, pointing her toward the hallway that led to her room. "It's that way. Can I help you with any bags?"

"That's quite all right," she answered. "I'll summon my equipment and tools when I'm in my room."

"You'll what?" Jack was a mortal and unaware of magicians' abilities to summon their possessions.

Dr. Hailey shook her head. "I didn't say anything. Anyway, I'll be off now. If you hear banging coming from the boiler room, it's only me fixing it."

"Okay." Jack watched the strange woman retreat.

Plato waited until the hotel owner disappeared into the kitchen before slinking out from the shadows. It was time to make some phone calls. Then the game would officially start.

CHAPTER EIGHT

Plato knew that Laura Ward practiced soccer on the lawn in front of the lagoon every afternoon. He waited until he heard the telltale *thud* on the rooftop of Hotel Laguna Maldita before sliding out of the shadows and briefly standing in the young girl's peripheral vision.

When she did a double-take, he hurried up the stairs that led to the three-story building's rooftop. Plato heard Laura running after him.

"Hey kitty," she called. "I won't hurt you."

Plato knew that was true. She also wasn't going to catch him. A few times, he heard the little soccer player slow down. He slowed then and waited for her to catch up. As soon as she came around the corner, he sped up several stairs, making progress to the rooftop.

Once at the top, Plato slid under a low lounge chair, completely out of sight. The rooftop was a nice place that guests couldn't utilize yet. There was some furniture, a gazebo, and grand views of the lagoon.

One unpaying guest currently occupied the space, although

he'd failed to check in since he was under the impression that he didn't have to.

Laura sped up the stairs and halted immediately, all color draining from her face when she took in the large magical creature before her. Her mouth popped open. Then it slammed shut, and she lifted a finger and pointed at the large blue dragon who appeared to be nesting on the roof of Hotel Laguna Maldita.

"Y-Yo-You're a dragon…" Laura stuttered.

Lunis pointed back at her, his eyes wide. "You're a little girl."

"Oh, my God." Laura stepped forward, then took two steps backward. "Are you going to eat me?"

"No." Lunis' expression turned offended. "I can't stand American food. You're American, right? Based on your accent, I'm guessing you are."

"Yes, I'm American." Laura didn't look relieved by the admission that the huge blue dragon wouldn't eat her based on her ethnicity.

"Now if you were Italian or French, well, then I might eat you," Lunis stated.

"What are you doing here?" Laura's confidence grew. "Do you live here? Did we buy a hotel with a dragon? Do I own you now?"

Lunis gave her a confused look. "No, no one can own me, but don't tell my rider, Sophia, that. No, I live in Beverly Hills—"

"That's an odd place for a dragon to live," Laura interrupted.

"Well, I split my time with our summer castle in Scotland," Lunis explained. "No, I'm vacationing here because I got this." He presented an embossed piece of stationary. Laura was hesitant to approach the dragon and take the note, although she did.

Her eyes ran over the fancy print before reading aloud,

"Lunis, you are cordially invited to enjoy a week at the all-inclusive Hotel Laguna Maldita in beautiful Tortugas Locas. Due to your service for the Dragon Elite and Rogue Riders, the Ward family would like to pamper you to ensure you can continue to protect our globe. Please find

your accommodations on the rooftop of the hotel. Meals will be delivered around the clock, and all your needs and expectations met. We hope you enjoy your stay."

Laura glanced up after reading the card, complete confusion on her face. "You're Lunis?"

"That I am," he answered proudly. "I'm excited to meet the Ward family who will be pampering me and honoring my service to the planet."

"I'm Laura Ward, but my family didn't send this."

Lunis lowered his chin. Smoke issued from his nostrils. "Say what?"

"Yeah, my mother and father, well, they're struggling to keep the hotel going. So they wouldn't have sent this," Laura said. "Although we've heard dragons are real, we didn't believe it. I didn't until now. So there's no way my father would've sent this to you. Or even known where to send it."

"So this is a trap," Lunis muttered as if he was off-put. "No wonder there are no pillows or high thread-count comforters up here. Can we change that?"

"You said it was a trap." Laura suddenly looked around. "Why would you stay?"

"Well, because if someone lured me here, I want to meet this guy and he can meet my flame. Also, my rider Sophia is off on a solo mission or something. Therefore I have some spare time to kill...not you. I won't kill you...probably...maybe...most likely not."

Laura giggled. "So you're staying?"

"Are you getting me pillows and meals around the clock?" Lunis asked.

"Well, I don't know." Laura deflated. "I might get in trouble. Maybe if my parents know—"

"You can't tell your parents," Lunis interrupted.

"I can't lie to them."

"No, you can't. But something is awry here. I've been brought here for a reason and the less who know about me, the better."

"Well, what if my dad comes up here and finds you? I mean, no one ever comes up here, but what if he does?"

"So if no one comes up here, then why did you?" Lunis asked.

"Oh, I saw this strange cat and followed him," Laura said at once and looked around. "I don't know where he went."

"A cat, you say…" Lunis gazed around the rooftop, but Plato knew he wouldn't see him hiding under the low chair. "Was this cat black and white, perchance?"

"He was!" Laura exclaimed.

"Nice work, Plato," Lunis sang, narrowing his eyes. "So what is it you want me to do?"

"Say what?" Laura asked.

"You said your family is struggling to keep the hotel open." Lunis settled down on the rooftop, getting comfortable. "Tell me more, Laura Ward. Tell me all the pertinent details."

"Oh, well, we just bought this place," Laura explained. "My mother is from Mexico and a great chef. My dad has always dreamed of owning and operating a small hotel. So they jumped on this opportunity."

"But you don't like it here." Lunis picked up on the regret in her tone.

"Well, I don't have any friends here."

Lunis nodded. "But your mother is from Mexico, so this means a lot to her."

"Yeah, I guess." Laura kicked the rooftop.

"Hey, do you know what you call a Mexican with a rubber toe?" Lunis suddenly looked serious.

Laura glanced up, confused. "What? Huh?"

"Roberto!"

The young girl blinked at him. "Was that a joke?"

Lunis huffed. "If this is going to work, you have to know when I'm telling a joke."

"If what's going to work?"

"Me swooping in and saving the hotel from whatever it needs saving from," Lunis stated.

Laura shrugged. "I don't know. I mean, we don't really have any customers, well, except those mean guys who bullied Dad earlier."

Lunis paused her, holding up a single talon like a finger. "Back up. Tell me about these guys."

"Oh, well, Dad called them mobsters or something," Laura explained. "They aren't going to pay for rooms and threatened him. I don't know..."

"Keep going," Lunis urged.

"Well, then there's the weird noises the boiler makes," she continued. "It makes it difficult to sleep at night. Mom thinks something's haunting the hotel. Dad says that she's exhausted and sleep-deprived. Anyway, the noise should be gone soon because a scientist showed up today. She's staying at the hotel and offered to fix the boiler for us."

"Interesting," Lunis mused.

"Is it?" Laura asked. "I don't know. I think we should move back and give up this dream of living in Mexico."

"Yeah, maybe." Lunis suddenly looked up. "Oh, hey. That reminds me. Do you know why the Mexican couldn't practice archery?"

Confusion resurfaced on Laura's face. "What?"

"Because he didn't habanero." Lunis laughed at his joke.

Laura caught the punch line and let out an easy laugh. "Oh, that was funny."

"Of course it was," he said coolly. "Oh, did you hear about the Mexican train killer? He had a locomotive."

Laura laughed harder. "You're really funny. I can't believe I met a dragon *and* he tells jokes."

"Awesome jokes," Lunis added.

"So you're going to stay?" Laura asked.

"Are you going to feed me?"

"Will you tell me awesome jokes?"

"You couldn't stop me even if you wanted to," he stated. "Believe me. Many have tried and failed."

"You think there's something here you need to save us from?" Laura cautiously looked around.

"It sounds like there's a lot of suspicious activity," Lunis answered. "If Plato set this up, well, it's probably one of the most important missions I'll attend to this year."

"Then maybe I can find you something soft to sleep on." Laura pointed at where he was lying on tattered patio cushions.

"I prefer bamboo sheets and organic down comforters," he supplied.

She scrunched up her nose. "I might be able to get some light blankets from one of the unused rooms."

"Deal," Lunis chirped.

"How about I go and get you something from the kitchen to eat?" Laura offered. "I think Mom made some extra roast beef since we have more guests tonight."

"I think this is going to be the start of a beautiful partnership."

"Me too." The young girl headed for the stairs and retreated at once.

Plato disappeared from his hiding spot, happy about putting another piece on his side of the chessboard.

CHAPTER NINE

From the cracked door of the pantry, Plato had a perfect view of the kitchen. He watched from the shadows as the chef of Hotel Laguna Maldita hurried around making dinner and generally stressing over her difficult situation.

Francesca blotted the sweat off her forehead. Yes, it was hot in her kitchen since she had six pots on the stovetop, three roasts in the oven, and tortillas on the griddle. However, she'd be sweating even if it wasn't hot in the kitchen or Tortugas Locas. It was the stress all around her making things feel like they were simmering.

The mob guys had set up in the lobby and were ordering Jack around nonstop. Anytime he refused them something, they made threats. Francesca told him it was better to give them what they wanted. They didn't need trouble.

Then there was the boiler spontaneously making startling noises, putting Francesca even more on edge. On top of all that, Francesca wasn't sleeping very well, firmly believing that an angry ghost was terrorizing the hotel at night and sometimes during the day.

Lifting a spoon from a simmering pot of beans, she blew on it and took a small taste. "Oh, it needs more paprika."

Absentmindedly, she reached over without looking to the spot where she kept her herbs. To her surprise, when she glanced at the shaker she'd retrieved, it was paprika. Sprinkling a bit into the pot, Francesca stirred the beans before tasting them again.

"More cumin," she said. Again, she reached into the area with herbs, glancing the other way over her shoulder at a commotion coming from the dining area. The mobsters were getting rowdier as they got comfortable there.

Once more, to her surprise, she'd picked the right spice shaker from the mix. Francesca sprinkled some cumin into the pot and tasted. "Oh, it needs a smidge of oregano."

She stirred the pot, reaching for the herbs.

"You're all out of oregano," a squeaky voice said from the countertop.

Francesca spun and jumped back several feet, her wooden spoon in her hands like a weapon. She blinked, taking in the sight of the talking squirrel sitting on her countertop. Faraday, the squirrel who was excellent at science and a devoted friend to many, held up an empty spice shaker.

He shook it. "See? You're out of oregano."

Francesca closed her eyes tight. "Dear God. I'm hallucinating. Please help me."

"What did you see?" Faraday looked around the kitchen for something dangerous.

Francesca opened her eyes and blinked at the squirrel. "It's you. You're a figment of my imagination. You can talk."

He nodded. "Yeah, a science experiment that went wrong…or one might say, very right. Anyway, I can talk. You can cook. My name is Faraday. And you are…"

"Francesca," she supplied.

"We're all caught up then." Faraday smiled. "We can get to my first lesson."

"First lesson?" She tilted her head in confusion.

"Yeah, for my internship in Mexican cooking." He picked up an embossed card sitting on the countertop next to him and held it out for her.

With a shaking hand, she reached forward and grabbed it from the squirrel as if he might suddenly turn rabid and bite her.

Her eyes ran over the raised print before she began reading out loud,

"Faraday, you are cordially invited to learn the art of Mexican cuisine from the world-renowned chef at Hotel Laguna Maldita in beautiful Tortugas Locas. Due to your and Paris Beaufont's devotion to your farm-to-table restaurant, Little Pleasures, the Ward family would like to gift you with this opportunity to advance your culinary knowledge. Please meet with your instructor in the kitchen and be prepared to learn from the very best. Your accommodations and meals are included during your stay. We hope you enjoy your time with us."

She lowered the card with pure confusion on her face. "I didn't send this."

"You're the chef at Hotel Laguna Maldita?" Faraday asked.

She nodded. "Francesca Ward."

"You're an expert in Mexican cuisine?"

"I guess…I mean, I'm not sure about expert. You have a farm-to-table restaurant? You're a talking squirrel." This information was still hard for Francesca to digest. It was obvious.

"Yes, and my sidekick is a fairy godmother of sorts." Then he added, "Although I believe Paris thinks of me as her sidekick. Don't tell her it's the other way around."

Francesca mopped her brow with a cloth. "Oh my. Fairy godmothers, talking squirrels, mobsters, and ghosts…I can't take anymore."

"Did you say mobsters and ghosts?"

She nodded and pointed toward the dining room, where the

commotion was getting louder. "Yeah, they took over the hotel today. Then the ghost...well, my husband says it's the boiler acting up, but I think it's an upset ghost."

"I could take a look at the boiler if you'd like," Faraday offered.

"You're a squirrel," she countered.

"A science experiment that went right, remember. I know things."

"And you cook," Francesca added.

"Well, no one else could take the internship opportunity when you sent it, so I was elected."

"I didn't send it."

"Right," Faraday chirped. "Someone lured me here. It sounds like you need help. Maybe I'll stick around for a bit and keep an eye on things. Paris is on a solo mission suddenly and doesn't need my help. So I might as well offer you my expertise. Like that boiler, for instance."

Francesca waved him off. "A scientist checked into the hotel today and offered to take a look at it today."

"Today...a scientist..." Faraday flicked his tail, thinking. "Yeah, I'll need to look into this."

"No one can see you running around this place," Francesca said in a mad rush. "I mean, if anyone reported that we have rodents, well, that's a huge problem. Then if someone sees a talking squirrel...well, we already have a ghost."

"Leave it to me, Francesca. No one will see me. I'm the master of stealth. If you have a problem with your boiler or a ghost, I'll find out immediately and help you."

"You will?" She suddenly softened. "But why? Why help us?"

He smiled. "Because you seem like a good person, trying to follow your passion. And someone led me here to help you. I don't know why or how, but my instinct tells me that I should trust it."

"That's a very odd thing for a squirrel to say," she admitted after a long pause.

"I assure you that I almost never say what you'd expect a squirrel to say."

"Which is nothing at all," she added with a forced laugh.

Faraday laughed too.

Plato disappeared from the dark pantry, having put the last chess piece on the board. It was finally time to start playing the game. He only hoped that he'd set everything up perfectly because now he was out of the game and relying on his rook, bishop, and knight, hoping they were all ready to checkmate the other player's king.

CHAPTER TEN

From his spot in a recess in the lobby wall, Plato posed like a statue, watching the events unfolding in Hotel Laguna Maldita. Overnight, the rumbling in the walls hadn't stopped. If anything, it had grown worse, as if the boiler was about to explode.

The mobsters were allowing the power to go to their heads. The strange scientist, Dr. Hailey, bobbed around the hotel while talking to herself and snapping at anyone who inquired what she was talking about.

"Waiter." Donte snapped from his table. "Get me another drink. When my client gets here, don't wait on us. I don't want you overhearing our important business."

Fishy Paul leaned in. "Is this one with the head of the transportation committee? Are we pushing our rule down on them?"

Donte's nostrils flared. "I swear, you're worthless. Go back there to the kitchen and find out what's taking so long with my tacos."

Fishy Paul didn't argue. He trudged for the kitchen at once.

"Yes, sir," the brand-new waiter said. Jack had hired him that morning, realizing that they would need extra help if things continued that way. The waiter, named Emmanuel, bowed slightly and headed back to the bar.

"What if the taxi drivers won't give you part of their profits for our protection?" Gruesome Kevin asked.

"Then we'll threaten to demolish their fleet of cars and throw our support behind the Uber and Lyft drivers," Donte answered at once. "All you have to do is find a man's weakness, and you can bring him down at the knees."

"Does it ever keep you up at night that we make our money off other people's hard work?" Gruesome Kevin asked, quite seriously.

Donte flinched, his hand flexing by his side. "No," he finally answered. "What kept me up last night was that incessant howling from the boiler. That thing needs to get fixed, or I'm taking it out with my best friend." He patted his holstered gun.

"The owners have assured me that the boiler is under repair," Emmanuel stated, delivering a drink to Donte. "In the meantime, Mr. Ward has offered earplugs to any of the hotel's guests."

"Whatever." Donte shooed the waiter away. "My first victim… I mean, client is here. Clear off and ensure nothing interrupts us."

"But Donte," Gruesome Kevin cut in. "The lobby is for hotel guests."

"If not for us, this place won't have any guests," Donte said in a stern tone, turning his attention back to Emmanuel. "As I said, no one is allowed in here during our meetings. Not even the Wards. See to it."

"Very well, sir." The waiter bowed and backed away.

Plato's eyes narrowed, watching the scene unfold before him. It might've appeared to many that the mobsters were taking over and everything was out of control, but to the magical lynx, everything was going perfectly to plan.

CHAPTER ELEVEN

There were many places in the boiler room for Plato to hide, but it was the area where he'd be least likely to be spotted. There were so many things happening in the cramped space that no one would notice him in the corners watching.

When Dr. Beth Hailey entered the room a moment later, her attention was on the large, rusty boiler that didn't appear to be having any problems at all.

Greedily, she rubbed her hands together. "Oh, you're perfect. Aren't you? All I have to do is remove a few of your major pieces, and I'll have what I need for the hurricane machine."

Something loud *thudded* overhead. Dr. Hailey looked up at the ceiling and narrowed her eyes. "Oh, selfish guests being loud. You all kept me up all night. Unthoughtful jerks."

Pulling a wrench from her coat, Dr. Hailey made her way over to the boiler. Another loud jolt rocked the boiler room. However, the scientist was smart enough to realize that the commotion wasn't coming from the machinery itself. "This place is old and probably built on a fault line. I better hurry before a big earthquake hits."

She went straight to work, stripping the boiler of essential parts. There had been nothing wrong with the old boiler at Hotel Laguna Maldita before. However, after Dr. Hailey finished with it, then it would be unusable and in need of replacing. The Ward family would have other things to worry about at that point, though.

A howl shot through the boiler room, and with it, a freezing chill like the area was suddenly a walk-in freezer. Dr. Hailey shot to a standing position, looking around both sides of her.

"Is someone there? Show yourself," she demanded.

Another deep howl met her order.

The scientist shook her head. "Stupid old building full of drafts and odd noises. I can't wait to be out of this dump. First, I'll have to test the hurricane machine, and in doing so, I'll probably demolish the exterior of this rundown place. Oh well, not my problem. When I get paid, I'm getting a place in Monte Carlo and not dealing with hovels like this ever again."

Another howl shot through the air, cutting off Dr. Hailey's crazy speech. She shook her head and got back to work, stripping the boiler's essential parts. Soon the guests and residents of Hotel Laguna Maldita would be out of hot water, but that would be the least of their concerns.

Plato knew that the problem keeping everyone awake had never been the boiler. It had always been the ghost that haunted the hotel. He was madder than hell, and about to take his rage out on the place he once called home. The only thing worse than the angry ghost was the storm that would soon rock the foundation of Hotel Laguna Maldita.

Hiding in small, dark places was nothing new for Plato. He'd been doing it for all his very long life. One reason, he learned early on, was that observing was an underappreciated superpower. What people did when they thought no one was watching was very revealing. Yes, most considered it creepy to monitor people without their knowledge, but for Plato, the standards were different.

As one of the most powerful entities on the planet, Plato had a moral obligation to observe and intervene in the world's affairs. If he weren't watching from the shadows and acting accordingly, many bad things would've happened in the world's history.

Also, Plato's magic, although incredibly powerful and seemingly limitless, had one crucial caveat. If someone observed him using it, he lost a life. Having a hundred lives might seem like a lot, but one could go through those rapidly if they weren't careful. Plato had already done that once. He was currently on his second round of lives, and he wasn't about to waste them by performing magic where others could witness it.

From under the low chair on the rooftop, Plato watched in the darkness as Faraday snuck up the gutter. The talking squirrel peeked over the edge, peering around. What he saw appeared somewhat ordinary. Sitting on the Hotel Laguna Maldita's roof was a cluster of patio furniture draped in a tarp to protect it from the storm brooding overhead.

However, Faraday was prepared and had a small monocle he could use to investigate the situation further. He lifted the magitech lens he'd created to his small eye and peered through.

The squirrel snickered. "As I suspected… You can take down your glamour, Lunis. I see you."

The special lens that Faraday was using could see through glamour. As he'd suspected, the blue dragon was using it to hide in case one of the guests or employees came up there.

Almost at once, the patio furniture image disappeared, replaced by the large blue dragon. Lunis was grinning.

"Well, hey there, Faraday. Did you win an all-inclusive vacation to this place too?"

The squirrel shook his head, climbing over the ledge and scurrying closer to the dragon. The pair had worked together on other missions, and as Beaufonts, knew each other quite well.

"No, I received an internship to learn Mexican cooking," he explained. "Surprisingly, I didn't apply for the opportunity. How about you?"

"Yeah, it was like the package dropped magically into my lap." Lunis sniffed the air. "Do you smell a rat?"

"More like a feline." Faraday snickered.

"How did you know I was up here?" Lunis asked.

"Well, although Laura is growing, I didn't buy that the twelve-year-old ate an entire rack of lamb. That's what she tried to convince her mother of when it went missing."

Lunis licked his chops. "That rack of lamb was delicious."

"Then I put together that someone lured me here. I believe it was Plato," Faraday continued.

The blue dragon nodded. "Oh, yes, this whole situation reeks of the magical lynx."

"I figured that if Plato lured me here to solve the goings-on, he might've also secretly recruited you."

"Yes, dear Watson, I think your observation is accurate."

Faraday grimaced at the dragon and crossed his tiny arms. "Why do you get to be Sherlock Holmes in this scenario?"

"Isn't it obvious?"

"Not really," Faraday said grumpily.

"Because I smoke a pipe." Lunis held up an imaginary pipe to his mouth and blew out smoke rings.

The squirrel laughed. "That's the other way I figured you out. Francesca said that she kept smelling a bonfire when tidying up the lawn area and hearing a flapping sound."

"Hey, you didn't expect me to eat the rack of lamb raw. I'm a dragon, not a savage."

Faraday nodded. "So you smoked it. That makes sense."

"I have a related question for you." Lunis hid a grin.

"I'm certain you don't," the squirrel replied dryly.

"If we are what we eat, does that make you nuts?"

Faraday didn't laugh. Instead, he shook his head. "I saw that joke coming a mile away. You know I'm allergic to nuts."

"Right, because that's not weird for a squirrel."

"I talk," Faraday countered. "That's what makes me weird."

"Plus that whole science thing you do." Lunis indicated the monocle hanging from Faraday's neck.

"Yes, and I've deduced that my science background is one of the reasons Plato enlisted my help," Faraday explained. "There's a nutty magitech scientist who I discovered stripping the boiler of essential parts. From what I've observed, she's trying to create a machine that generates a hurricane."

Lunis looked up at the brooding storm clouds overhead. "Looks like she might be succeeding. Did you recognize the machine she's working on? Is that how you know she intends to create a hurricane?"

Faraday shook his head. "No, the nutter talks to herself incessantly. She pretty much disclosed that some man hired her to build the machine. Doctor Beth Hailey doesn't plan on creating the full hurricane, but her testing has created a potential storm. I suspect it will only get worse."

Lunis huffed. "Oh, great. Maybe I can get a room inside the hotel."

"I doubt it. That's the other problem brewing in the hotel. Have you heard about the mobsters who have taken over in there?"

"Yeah, Laura told me about them."

Faraday nodded. "Yeah, their wrath is getting worse, and the family is suffering. They intimidate all the guests and make a lot of unreasonable demands."

"The greedy little jerks need to be taught a lesson."

Faraday flicked his tail. "I agree. Then, on top of that, I think a ghost is haunting the hotel.

"Jack thinks the malfunctioning boiler is the cause of the incessant knocking in the noises in the walls. However, the boiler didn't have any problems until Dr. Hailey started stripping parts from it. As Francesca said, I've noticed objects fly off shelves and the exterior walls shaking."

"Which wouldn't be the case if it were a boiler issue," Lunis mused, combing his claws over his chin like a detective thinking on a case.

"Yes, so I thought that maybe we could do some research on Hotel Laguna Maldita," Faraday began. "The family doesn't know anything about the place. Neither one of us can quiz the locals to get information."

"Because talking squirrels and dragons freak mortals out," Lunis cut in.

"Exactly," Faraday chirped. "So I can take a trip to the Great Library and see if Paul, the Great Librarian, can help me find history on this place. If someone recorded it, then it would be there."

Lunis gauged the dark clouds overhead again. "You better hurry on that one because something tells me that we don't have long."

Plato flicked his white-tipped tail twice from his hiding spot. An old leather-bound book appeared to the side of the two magical creatures, followed by a *popping* sound. They both swung around, looking alert. Their eyes darted to the book sitting on the rooftop.

Faraday arched an eyebrow at Lunis. "That book wasn't there a moment ago, was it?"

"I don't believe so, dear Watson."

"Again, why do you get to be Sherlock?" Faraday complained. "You tell too many bad jokes to be the great detective."

"Just for that, I'm not entertaining you with any of my jokes, and you pronounced awesome wrong."

Lunis made his way over to the book in one step while Faraday scurried in several hops. The blue dragon leaned over the tome, flipping to a marked page. His eyes widened at once. "Watson. Come at once if convenient. If inconvenient, come all the same."

Faraday hurried around to the other side of the book, which the large blue dragon mostly blocked. It appeared to be a history of Tortugas Locas. "So you've given up jokes to quote Sherlock Holmes now? How do you know those?"

Lunis looked up from the book and winked at him. "My name is Sherlock Holmes. It is my business to know what other people don't know."

Faraday laughed at this. "Wow, I set you up perfectly for that."

Lunis tapped the book with his claw. "Look at this. It's the history of Hotel Laguna Maldita."

Faraday scanned the words as he muttered, "Built in...duh... duh...duh..." He skipped down several passages. "The ownership traded hands several times...duh...duh...duh..."

"Wow, take a speed-reading class." Lunis laughed and pointed at the bottom of the page with his sharp claw. "Down here is the story of our ghost, I believe." He cleared his throat and began to read from the book.

"A baron by the name of Fabien Coulter stole his family's fortune, enraging his six older brothers. Fabien escaped to Tortugas Locas to 'live like a king' and elude being hunted down by his siblings. He moved into Hotel Laguna Maldita and lived a lavish lifestyle with dozens of servants, famous guests, and rich foods.

"However, it didn't last for long. The Coulter brothers tracked him down, retrieved the stolen riches, locked him in his hotel, surrounded it, and declared that if he tried to leave, one of the brothers would kill him on the spot. Left with nothing but his hotel and bare rations, Fabien Coulter lasted ten days before taking his life."

Faraday's chin jerked up, his eyes wide. "It's the baron who haunts the hotel. That makes perfect sense."

"It appears that this saved you the time and trouble of going to the Great Library for research."

"Yes, thanks, Plato," Faraday called over his shoulder.

Lunis snickered. "In truth, I think the one who is playing the real Sherlock Holmes is that magical lynx."

"I suspect you're correct," Faraday mused. "So we have a mad scientist creating a hurricane, a boiler that's about to blow, three mobsters creating trouble, and an angry ghost. I see why Plato recruited our help, but how do you suppose he expects us to fix all these problems?"

"There is nothing more deceptive than an obvious fact." Lunis pretended to smoke a pipe again.

"Would you stop quoting Sherlock Holmes and say what you mean?" Faraday insisted.

"We could take each of our three villains down," Lunis began.

"I'm confident that we could. Or we could use them to take each other down."

Faraday gasped. "Yes! Of course, that would be a Plato strategy. Why fight your enemies when you can make them fight each other?"

"Elementary, my dear Watson." Lunis winked at the squirrel.

Faraday tapped his paw against his chin while thinking. "Okay, I think I have a plan that could pen our villains together and get rid of them before they create too much trouble."

Lunis leaned close. "Okay, I'm ready to hear your plan and take full credit for its brilliance."

Faraday chuckled before whispering his ideas to the blue dragon. Plato smiled, realizing that he'd enlisted the right creatures for this case. As Sherlock Holmes would've said, "We balance probabilities and choose the most likely. It is the scientific use of the imagination."

CHAPTER THIRTEEN

Gale-force winds bent the palm trees in front of the lagoon and made coconuts drop to the ground like large bits of hail. The waves in the lagoon rose high over the retaining wall, flooding the lawn. The rain that had started as a sprinkle quickly turned into a torrential downpour.

The hurricane had officially started, Plato observed from the shelter of a hotel window. Dr. Hailey's testing had quickly gotten out of control. What the mad scientist didn't realize was that one can't create a little storm. Once the conditions were right, the forces of nature took over.

In her efforts to test the hurricane machine, Dr. Hailey had created one, and it would have to run its course. However, as Sherlock Holmes once said, "Not all storms come to disrupt your life. Some come to clear your path."

That was precisely Plato's plan. This storm would do more than some wind damage to Hotel Laguna Maldita. If everything went as designed, it would clear the place out for a brand-new beginning.

Francesca and Jack hurried to furl the umbrellas and pull in the lawn furniture before they blew away. The storm had broken so suddenly that it gave them little time to prepare. They'd ordered Laura to stay inside the hotel's safety, but thanks to Lunis, she had a vital job.

Plato glanced at the hotel bar where the young girl was pretending to do her math homework. A few neighborhood cats had taken shelter in the hotel's lobby due to the storm, so no one noticed Plato. He enjoyed not having to hide for once, which would make observing the next chess moves easier.

No one gave an unassuming black and white cat much attention with all the craziness going on. And no one would suspect that he was orchestrating all the events that would come to pass.

"Emmanuel." Laura tapped her pencil on her notebook. "Did you hear about the ship that's docking here in Tortugas Locas during the storm?"

"Huh, what?" the waiter asked from behind the bar, looking around absentmindedly.

"Yeah, apparently it's a cargo ship with diamonds that never makes a stop between its destinations." Laura chewed on her pencil and recited her script perfectly.

Donte overheard and looked up from his usual table. "Hey Lori, what's that about a diamond ship?"

The twelve-year-old turned on her stool at the bar and scowled at the mobster. She was the only one of the Wards who wasn't afraid of Donte or his goons. "My name is Laura. I was talking to Emmanuel, not you."

Unused to be talked back to and especially not by a young girl, Donte looked flustered for a moment before shaking it off. "Well, I want you to talk to me."

She rolled her dark brown eyes. "Fine, there's this ship. It's called *The Tiffany*, and apparently, the unexpected storm is forcing it to dock here. Usually, it doesn't have stops, but it's not safe to be out at sea right now, so it's mooring in the harbor."

Donte narrowed his eyes at Laura. "How'd you find out about this?"

"My math teacher told us," Laura answered right on cue, completely unfazed. "Her husband works in the shipping yard and said that the boat's size was greater than they typically handle. Then she made up this whole geometry lesson on how to navigate the ship into the harbor. I guess it was supposed to be a practical lesson, but all I could think of was how cool it would be to go aboard and see all those diamonds."

"Yeah, cool." Donte turned back to Gruesome Kevin and Fishy Paul. Both were giving him eager looks.

Laura, still acting, turned back to her homework. "Well, unfortunately, I won't get a chance because the ship is only here until the storm passes."

"Plus, you're a kid who isn't allowed on a ship full of diamonds," Emmanuel added, polishing a glass.

"Yeah, there's that." Laura smiled at Plato as he passed on his way to the boiler room.

CHAPTER FOURTEEN

Plato passed two alley cats that had taken refuge in Hotel Laguna Maldita on the way to the boiler room. They were very much acting like cats and not spying like him. Without being noticed, Plato slipped into the boiler room to find Dr. Hailey in the state he expected—completely losing her mind.

Her red hair was in her hands, and she was regarding the hurricane machine with a vengeance. The force and magic issuing from the device had been enough that they blew out the bank of windows along one wall. That was when the magical hurricane had entered the atmosphere, cycling until it built up and became a real storm.

Wind and sprays of water shot into the open space. The howling from the storm made it almost impossible to hear the raging scientist.

"You weren't supposed to do this!" Dr. Hailey pulled her hair and ran around the large machine she'd created beside the now broken boiler. The scientist had stripped the boiler, and now no one would be taking a warm shower. However, most would think that was because of the hurricane approaching the shores.

"It was supposed to be a test!" the redhead yelled, throwing her hands at the machine that *hissed* in reply.

The one who seemed more likely to have a conversation was the baron beating on the walls. Dr. Hailey swung around and regarded the bricks of the exterior wall. "There are no boiler issues. So what's making that noise?"

Right on cue, as if he was waiting to be invited out, a ghostly face pooled through the bricks. His eyes were sunken. His light-colored hair came to his chin, and he wore a regal outfit befitting a ninth-century French nobleman. However, his transparent white appearance made it obvious that he hadn't been in this world for a very long time.

"You dare to terrorize my home?" Baron Fabien Coulter boomed, his mouth wide and voice echoing,

Dr. Beth Hailey screamed. Her hands flew into her hair, and her eyes widened in horror. "You're a-a-a ghost!"

"And you're dead!" Baron Fabien Coulter threatened, his hands extended as though he was going to strangle the scientist.

Her screams blended into the howling storm winds as Dr. Hailey ran for the busted-out windows. She dove out of the boiler room, rolled onto the soaked lawn, and raced into the storm, heading straight for the lagoon. The winds battered her, but the ghost halted short of leaving the hotel that imprisoned him.

CHAPTER FIFTEEN

Plato caught sight of something curious through the broken boiler room window. He disappeared and reappeared under the shelter of a boathouse. It was adjacent to the small dock that belonged to Hotel Laguna Maldita, where they tied up their small jet boat. The storm had moved in so fast that Jack hadn't a chance to secure the craft. It currently bobbed furiously in the water.

The magical lynx peeked out of a storage closet and spied as the three strode over to the small dock. They'd flipped up their jacket collars to shield them from the driving rain.

"Donte, do you think it's safe to go out in this storm?" The wind and rain distorted Fishy Paul's voice.

"No!" Donte called, jumping down into the boat, which had taken on water. "But you heard. We only have until the storm ends to get to *The Tiffany*. Now help me bail out."

"But Donte, we can't carry that many diamonds in a boat this size," Gruesome Kevin complained, clumsily jumping into the small craft.

"All we need is to fill our pockets, boys." Donte started the engine. Oddly enough, the keys had been in plain sight on the front desk counter. He didn't question it.

The goons were still throwing buckets of water over the sides when Donte reversed and sped out toward the harbor, inexpertly trying to power through the hurricane-whipped waves.

Plato glanced up into the sky as the large blue dragon launched off Hotel Laguna Maldita's roof and soared through the air, undeterred by the storm winds and rain. He raced easily after the boat that would hopefully never make it to *The Tiffany*.

CHAPTER SIXTEEN

Plato materialized back in the boiler room, his job now to keep an eye on things. The events that unfolded at this point were mostly like a movie for his entertainment. It was highly entertaining to watch his friends spring into action.

Faraday was where Plato had expected. The squirrel was working furiously on the hurricane machine. The wind that raced around the device took the little rodent off his feet several times, but he managed to jump to a safe place and get back to work.

The baron's ghost hadn't cooled down after chasing off Dr. Hailey. He appeared even more enraged than before, screaming as he beat his chest. The volume of his voice shook the hotel's foundation, again throwing Faraday off-balance.

The little squirrel dove to avoid debris that flew in from the storm. He found a safe place on the machine's far side, where he continued his tinkering.

"My home has been invaded!" Baron Fabien Coulter exclaimed. "I won't put up with it any longer! If I can't live in peace here, no one will. I'll demolish the place."

Plaster shook from the walls. A crack ran up the bricks to the ceiling. Overhead, it sounded like the roof was going to cave in.

Faraday glanced around the hurricane machine with a nervous look in his eyes. "If you could give me one more minute? I have a surprise for you."

CHAPTER SEVENTEEN

Popping back to the boathouse storage closet, Plato spotted Lunis flying over the turbulent sea. The blue dragon swirled in the air around a cyclone of wind, debris, and water. It was a magnificent display of grace and strength.

On the ocean's surface, the small jet boat rose and dove with the high waves, barreling in the harbor's direction. What happened next was hard for Plato to make out, even with his enhanced senses. The storm was too heavy and blanketing to see through.

Still, Plato saw a blue wing out there. He heard the men in the boat yelling and saw fire. Then the wind and rain blasted him even in his hiding spot.

Still, the explosion on the lagoon's surface was clear. It rose high into the sky, a small but powerful mushroom cloud that stole attention from the storm, if only momentarily.

Plato glimpsed Lunis veering to the east, his wings flapping, and felt relief that the blue dragon was safe. The explosion meant he'd been successful, and the mobsters wouldn't create any more problems.

The lynx grinned with wicked delight, remembering a line from Sherlock Holmes. "I may be on the side of the angels…but don't think for one second that I am one of them."

CHAPTER EIGHTEEN

Confident that Lunis had taken care of the mobsters, Plato returned to the boiler room where things were heating up —figuratively and literally.

The temperature had risen by at least twenty degrees, and it had nothing to do with the storm beating against Hotel Laguna Maldita. It had everything to do with what Faraday, the scientific squirrel, had done to the hurricane machine.

The magitech that had created the storm currently waging war on the lagoon looked ready to burst. However, to Plato's relief, it appeared that Faraday had things under control even if he was scurrying around the machine pressing buttons and doing various science-type things.

The most important thing was that aside from the wind battering the hotel, the building was quiet. The shaking due to paranormal activity was gone. The howling due to a long-running haunting had stopped.

The ghost of Baron Fabien Coulter was gone. It was all thanks to what Faraday, the scientist squirrel had done.

Plato grinned, grateful that his friends had risen to the occasion to help him on his mission. The mobsters were gone. The mad scientist, too. And now the ghost that had terrorized Hotel Laguna Maldita for so long.

Plato snickered and headed out of the boiler room. No one could hear him over the commotion of the storm and the machinery. "To quote the great Sherlock Holmes, 'We all have a past. Ghosts. They are the shadows that define our every sunny day.'"

Turning for the warm hallway off the boiler room, Plato decided to look for a place to curl up and nap. He'd sleep off the storm and handle this mission's loose ends when it had passed, and the sun shone once more.

A tropical forest covered the lagoon area in Tortugas Locas that was closest to the airport. Plato appeared under the dark canopy off a sandy beach right before Dr. Beth Hailey washed up on shore, coughing and sputtering nonsense.

"Where am I?" The crazy woman shook her head of sodden red hair. "Is this Florida?"

She picked seaweed from her clothes, lurching as she crawled out of the waves. The storm had cleared and given way to a pristine blue sky and a peaceful breeze. Now, all that remained after the hurricane appeared to be washing up on the shores of Tortugas Locas—Dr. Hailey among it.

When the mad scientist made it to her feet, she looked down at her wet clothes and felt her body. "Who am I?"

She looked around with a crazed look in her eyes. "I don't remember who I am or where I've been..."

Plato knew that starting over was hard for most, but in some cases, it was much better than starting from where one used to be. To him, Dr. Hailey, or whatever she decided to call herself, had a fresh beginning. He sorely hoped she used her intelligence to do good this time rather than creating storms intended to destroy.

That was his final thought and wish for the scientist as she stumbled into the jungle, off to make a new life.

CHAPTER TWENTY

Plato enjoyed finding himself at the same warehouse where this adventure had started. From the shadows of the building and using his heightened senses, he watched the three men on the pier making a rushed exchange.

Donte looked like he'd seen a ghost. His black hair had a streak of white and his eyes were wide as he kept looking over his shoulder. "I've ordered a water taxi to pick me up here, and I don't want you two following me. I don't want to see either of you again."

"Don't worry about that," Gruesome Kevin said. "I've got a bike over there. I'm taking that as far as I can and hitchhiking from there."

"I got a job at the docks," Fishy Paul stated. "I found I don't mind the smell of fish, and with you two gone, I'll feel better."

"Yeah, but what about the boss?" Gruesome Kevin asked.

Donte shrugged. "Who cares. There are worse things out there than him."

"I believe we saw them." Fishy Paul looked like a ghost was suddenly haunting him as he stared into the murky waters of the harbor, all churned up after the storm.

Gruesome Kevin shivered. "I'm giving up crime."

Donte agreed, nodding as a small motorboat with the sign "Taxi" on the top pulled up to the dock. "Me too. After what I saw, I'm going straight."

"Okay, Donte." Fishy Paul nodded at him as he jumped down into the boat. "Take care and watch your back."

"You too, you two knuckleheads." Donte turned and waved at the other guys as the boat took off in the opposite direction. "Go make something of yourselves."

"Do you hear that?" Francesca asked her husband as she delivered a steaming hot cup of coffee on their hotel's patio.

Jack shook his head, listening to the gentle breeze whistling through the palm trees. "No, what is it?"

"Nothing!" she said triumphantly. "There's no knocking from the boiler or the angry ghost. The hotel is finally quiet."

He chuckled. "Oh, dear. I told you there was never any ghost."

"Oh, my friend Faraday said there was, but he's gone. Faraday also fixed the boiler." Francesca indicated the table in the corner where Plato sat with his friends Lunis and Faraday, drinking a bottle of whiskey.

"Crazy what the storm turned up." Jack glanced at the strange magical creatures. "Laura said the dragon was on the hotel's roof the entire time."

"Yeah, he helped run off those mobsters," Francesca explained.

"Your friend Faraday, that talking squirrel, he took care of the alleged ghost and the boiler and that weird scientist lady?" Jack asked.

"I think so," Francesca said. "Unfortunately, he says he has to return to his fairy godmother duties soon."

"My question," Jack began, "is what did that little black and white cat do?"

Francesca shrugged. "Maybe nothing. Maybe he's their friend."

"Yeah, maybe." Jack smiled at his wife and looked up at Hotel Laguna Maldita as his daughter rushed over with her soccer ball in hand. "I'm grateful that we can make a fresh beginning. I think this place is going to be great now."

"I agree." Laura threw her arms around her father and mother, wrapping them both in hugs.

CHAPTER TWENTY-TWO

"We did that." Lunis indicated the family hugging on the veranda.

"After hearing his story," Faraday cut in, "I think Plato did it."

"We do nothing alone," Plato stated, his eyes keen on the patrons in the hotel's lobby bar. They were all partying, even though the place was still in disarray after the storm. Many seemed enlivened as if the mobsters and ghost had terrorized them too and now were freed like the Wards.

"Waiter, can we get another bottle of whiskey?" Lunis asked Emmanuel as he passed.

"Another?" the waiter asked.

Lunis nodded. "I'm a dragon. I can drink enough for all of us."

"Plus, we have your story to hear," Faraday added. "We now know where Plato was when all the events were unfolding."

"We know that he was masterminding them," Lunis interrupted. "As I suspected."

"Yes, but now I want to know where you were, Lunis. How you came to be here and how you got rid of those goons." Faraday sipped his drink as the waiter came back with another bottle of Glenlivet.

"Okay, I'll tell you," Lunis said. "My story starts the same as Plato's. It all began three days ago..."

The lynx smiled inwardly as the dragon began his side of the story, which he already knew all too well. He was grateful that his friends could come together for the good of humanity. That's what the Beaufonts and their familiars did. Yes, Plato had masterminded all the events that had passed, but he couldn't do it without the bravery and expertise of the small and large friends next to him at the table.

It truly wasn't about the size of the hero. It was about the size of their hearts. None had bigger ones than Lunis and Faraday and the Beaufonts they belonged to.

Plato might've seemed small, but that in itself was the deception. As Sherlock Holmes once said, "To a great mind, nothing is little."

SARAH'S AUTHOR NOTES

OCTOBER 18, 2021

A huge thank you to all of you for reading our books, these short stories and putting up with my author notes. Thank you to all of the readers and the LMBPN team.

I wrote this short story for a few reasons. The first is that you, the readers, asked for a Plato story. See, I listen! Many of you asked for an origin story but you're not getting that because I don't know it…at least, not yet. Plato has many secrets he hasn't revealed, even to me.

Also, I wrote this story because I decided after finishing the Inscrutable Paris Beaufont series that I'd take a much needed break. But Mike and I didn't want to leave you high and dry.

I like to think that I'm a drug dealer, without all the shadiness and law breaking. My books are your drugs and you're always jonesing for them. Gotta get you your fix.

Anyway, Mike had the idea that during my break, I could write a few short stories to keep you all happy until I returned with the next series—The Unconventional Agent Beaufont. That was a good idea and would keep me in the habit of writing, while not requiring for me to work around the clock.

Here's what Sarah does: When given a break and an easy task, she overcomplicates it and makes it as difficult as possible. So I decided that instead of telling three short fun stories about magical creatures, I'd tell one very complex story told from three different perspectives. Talk about math, Batman.

I was having to chart all these different events and layout everything in graphs to keep track of things. I love seeing the same events told from different POVs, but I didn't want to bore you all. So that's why you don't see how the villains are defeated in Plato's story. You know they go down, but you don't know how. You have to read Lunis and Faraday's story to learn that. And small spoiler, there will be a twist at the end. The short stories all start and end at the bar. However, the final story will stretch to a new scene that happens afterwards. I can say no more.

I enjoyed writing this story much more than I expected. I have a playlist for each of my series that I listen to continuously throughout while writing them. I wrote The Unstoppable Liv Beaufont almost three years ago. Since this was Plato's story, I went back and listened to that old playlist and it was like time traveling. It stuck me right back in the days of writing Liv and Plato adventures. And you know what, I missed them so very much. It was like visiting old friends.

I really should get out more. It's just that I prefer my fictional characters to real people most of the time. Writing these short stories has given me extra time. Maybe I could socialize… That sounds exhausting. Instead I'm going to go and play the piano. Yes, in my time off, I'm learning piano. I posted a video of me practicing and you lovely readers were very encouraging, but don't worry, I'm not quitting my day job. Although I'd love to work at a piano bar someday. Dreams…

Mike, what untapped dreams do you have? Sky diving instructor? High school gym coach? Foreign Spy? Walmart Greeter?

Much love and Peace,
Tiny Ninja

81

MICHAEL'S AUTHOR NOTES

NOVEMBER 12, 2021

Thank you for not only reading this story but these author notes as well.

I am in Las Vegas for the 20Booksto50K® Vegas conference for indie authors, and I ran into Tiny Ninja™ a couple of times at the show.

For those of you who want to see Sarah talking to a crowd giving advice – the session is up on Youtube, and I was surprised to see she was taller than the podium.

Not by much… ;-)   https://youtu.be/JFS-u5lqU74

I was in Cannes, France, not that long ago, and Sarah wanted to TALK about these stories as she often does before a series. She failed to mention the whole timey-wimey thing she was involved in making happen with the short stories.

 As she mentioned, she failed 'easy reprieve on writing' 101.

(On a ZOOM call from France to California)

Mike: I'm sorry, you did what?

Sarah: I kind of complicated the three short stories and I'm not sure how to make 'x' happen in them.

Mike: Why?

Sarah: Why did I what?

Mike: Complicate them. Sarah, it was just three short stories about the support characters (animals) of the stories. How the @#%@# do you complicate that?

Mike: Uh huh...yes... right... OMG... You didn't REALLY? Oh...sh#%#! Sarah... WTH? Seriously? Right...Well...Uh... uh.... Uh...

... Look at the time... (It was something like 10:00 PM my time for this call.)

She and I worked through the challenges, and I'm very pleased with where Sarah decided to take the stories...*eventually*. There might have been heavy drinking involved.

A.O.S. (Angel On Shoulder) – *There was no heavy drinking involved unless you believe Coke is 'heavy' in which case yes – there was a lot of heavy drinking involved!*)

What untapped dream would do if I could do it?

Besides the choices Sarah provided (all good ones, no judgment here), I would have to say CEO of a Digital VR Based Entertainment Studio with a large budget (not self-funded) with total control (so yeah, some of my money must be involved) and the ability to drive the vision.

Oh...wait... I (kinda) have that now with LMBPN Studios. Wait...was I supposed to admit that so early?

;-)

Ad Aeternitatem,

Michael Anderle

THE FANTASTIC LUNIS

A BEAUFONT SHORT STORY BOOK 2

CHAPTER ONE

The battle might be over, but the destruction strewn around Hotel Laguna Maldita would long serve as reminders of the villains who'd tried to destroy it. Lunis, the majestic blue dragon, knew it was better if those in the coastal city of Tortugas Locas didn't let down their guard anyway. The storm might've passed, and the dangers sailed out to sea, but the truth was that the worst was yet to come.

Lunis knew that many guests were indiscreetly checking out him and his companions. The trio shared a table in the corner of the hotel bar. He understood, though. Mortals knew about magic, but it was still uncanny for most to see three talking, magical animals sharing a bottle of whisky in a hotel lobby. The excited guests kept gazing at them as they chatted and drank at the bar, not minding the damaged walls and furniture.

The family who owned Hotel Laguna Maldita were grateful to Lunis and Faraday, the talking squirrel, for helping them. However, they probably thought the black and white feline at their table was a regular cat. Plato was anything but ordinary. The story he'd shared of what he'd been doing while everything unfolded proved what Lunis and Faraday suspected—the lynx secretly brought them to Tortugas Locas to fight evil.

The large wrought iron chandelier that hung in the middle of the hotel's lobby was still intact, but recent events had knocked out many of its candles. Cracks in the plaster and broken paintings on the wall were reminders of the battle waged inside Hotel Laguna Maldita. The broken floor-to-ceiling windows that showed views of the now placid lagoon were shattered reminders of the fracas that had happened outside the hotel. Coconuts and debris were strewn across the lawn—all signs of the storm that had passed.

"Waiter, can we get another bottle of whiskey?" Lunis asked Emmanuel as he passed.

"Another?" the waiter confirmed.

Lunis nodded. "I'm a dragon. I can drink enough for all of us."

"Plus, we have your story to hear," Faraday added, indicating the blue dragon. "We now know where Plato was when all the events were unfolding."

"We know that he was masterminding them," Lunis interrupted. "As I suspected."

"Yes, but now I want to know where you were, Lunis. How you came to be here and how you got rid of those goons." Faraday sipped his drink as the waiter came back with another bottle of Glenlivet.

"Okay, I'll tell you." Lunis leaned forward and murmured, "My story starts the same as Plato's. It all began three days ago..."

CHAPTER TWO

Three Days Previously...

"I need a vacation." Lunis rolled onto his back and stared at the ceiling of his Pad. That was the name of his cave at the Gullington. Unlike the one where the other "boring" dragons resided at the Dragon Elite's headquarters in Scotland, his was beyond luxurious and designed with all his interests in mind. The groundskeeper for the Gullington, Quiet, had seen to it personally.

A large-screen television had access to all his favorite shows like *Community*, *The Magicians*, and *Sabrina the Teenage Witch*. He had every possible gaming system one could imagine. However, Lunis spent most of his free time playing Animal Crossing because it calmed his nerves after a tense mission.

A disco ball hung from the ceiling that complemented the thick shag rug on the floor. The cabinets along the wall held stocks of the blue dragon's favorite snacks like gummy worms, Doritos, and Reese's Pieces.

"What you need is spatial awareness," Sophia Beaufont

complained, trying to pull her leg out from under the huge dragon lying beside her...well, now on her. "You're on my boot and crushing my leg."

Lunis scoffed and shifted off her. "You know, I have feelings, right? No one likes to be called fat."

"You're a dragon who weighs a ton because you're huge and fly, carrying me through the skies." Sophia groaned and clutched her leg. "You're supposed to be heavy."

"You're a tiny human who's supposed to be weak." He rolled onto his stomach and propped his head on his clawed fists like a teenage girl. "Do you want me to point that out?"

"You're ridiculous, Lun."

"So no to a vacation then?" He pouted. "We saved the world from oversized termites."

"I think they were terrorists," Sophia corrected.

"Same thing," he muttered.

"I don't know." She rolled onto her stomach too and thought. "We need to get back to Beverly Hills to monitor the Rogue Riders. You know how they get unruly if I leave them unmonitored for long."

"Well, because you take a bunch of rebels and expect them to behave. They're going to need supervision, or they'll be crazy. So that's a 'no' to a bikini and cocktails then?"

"For you?" Sophia lowered her chin and regarded him with disgust. "You're never allowed to wear a bikini. And 'no' to vacation for right now."

"Fine," Lunis scoffed. "I'll go tell my suitcase the vacation is off." He sighed heavily. "Now I'll have emotional baggage."

Sophia shook her head and hid a laugh. "Oh wow. That was especially horrible."

"I know," he agreed. "I need a vacation. My jokes are all dried up."

"You have a home in Scotland and one in Beverly Hills and adventures all over the world. What else do you want?"

"Room service," he answered at once. "High thread counts on my Egyptian sheets. A nice view of a new body of water. Locals with fun accents. Tourists who have sunburns. You know, the usual."

Sophia laughed as her phone rang. "You're so weird."

"You're an appetizer," he retorted as she answered her phone.

A moment later, Lunis caught the tone of stress in Sophia's voice. She had an important call demanding her full attention, he knew at once. She rose to her feet, grabbed her unsheathed sword, and looked around for her cloak. He made to stand, but she waved him off while still on the phone and listening to directions.

That wasn't typical and meant he wouldn't be necessary. Lunis didn't like that, even if he wanted a long nap and some spicy Chinese delivery that night. Well, he would prefer to eat the Chinese delivery guy, but Sophia frowned upon such things so he usually settled for the dumplings.

"Okay, I'll be right there." Sophia ended the call.

Lunis directed his attention at her. "Where? Where are we going?"

"*We* aren't going anywhere." Sophia stressed the first word. "That was Papa Creola, and he needs my help with something."

"What? What does the Father of Time want with you? I'm much more entertaining."

She shook her head and slid her cloak over her shoulders. "I don't know entirely, but he said it was a stealth mission and that I should come alone and leave you behind."

Lunis looked offended. "I can be stealthy."

"Yes, and also wake the dead with your thundering footsteps and rumbling stomach," she retorted. "I'm sure I'm only doing reconnaissance, and I'll call you to my side once we have more details."

"We?" he questioned.

"Well, Liv is involved too," Sophia muttered while pulling her long blonde hair into a ponytail.

Lunis growled low in his throat. "I should've known that She-Who-Is-Intolerable was involved."

"Well, if it makes you feel any better, she's left Plato behind."

"Why would she do that? She's at a serious disadvantage without the lynx. Everyone knows that Liv is the sidekick and Plato is the real deal in the duo."

"No, I think no one knows that, and you want to believe it."

He shrugged. "She's the talker. I know Plato is the one who makes things happen."

"Well, regardless, this is a mission without familiars. I'll call you when I'm ready for your help."

"If I'm free, I'll see about helping when I get a chance."

Sophia laughed, walked over, and smiled up at the pouting dragon. "Come on, you know I always want you by my side. It's only that sometimes, I have to go it alone until it's time for your expertise and strength."

"So you're saying that I'm the wind beneath your wings?" he deadpanned.

Sophia giggled again and stood on tiptoe. He leaned down, and she gave him a peck on his cheek. "I'm saying that if I had wings, you would be. Since you do, how about I be the rider on your back."

"So you're saying that you're the pain in my backside then?" he joked. "That seems more accurate."

Sophia shook her head and made her way to the Pad's entrance. "I'll call you when I know more. Try not to get yourself into trouble. Don't stay up too late or eat too many sweets. And try to do some chores."

"Okay, Mom," he grumbled as she exited the cave. "Bring me back a souvenir from your adventures, which I wasn't invited to."

Lunis laid his head on the shag rug, feeling sorry for himself and his predicament although he wished he didn't. Pity wasn't the way of the dragons, but Lunis wasn't a typical dragon and usually felt emotions the others didn't.

He was about to close his eyes and decide on an early bedtime when something floated down from the ceiling and landed squarely on the floor in front of him, inches from his face.

CHAPTER THREE

An embossed piece of stationery appeared before him. He didn't tense from the thick card's sudden arrival out of seemingly nowhere. That was how things happened at the Gullington. Things appeared magically and also disappeared without warning. Quiet was usually responsible for such things. However, the card didn't seem like the work of the tiny gnome who hardly spoke.

Lunis' eyes ran over the fancy print on the cream-colored card before he read aloud,

"Lunis, you are cordially invited to enjoy a week at the all-inclusive Hotel Laguna Maldita in beautiful Tortugas Locas. Due to your service with the Dragon Elite and Rogue Riders, the Ward family would like to pamper you to ensure you can continue to protect our globe. Please find your accommodations on the hotel's rooftop. Meals will be available around the clock, and all your needs and expectations met. We hope you enjoy your stay."

He looked up suddenly, then glanced over his shoulder as if he expected someone to be there. No one was. It was uncanny that he'd wanted to go on a vacation and this unexpected invitation appeared.

"This might be a trick." He was used to talking to himself since he enjoyed his jokes the best of anyone. Sophia liked them but pretended not to, and he preferred it that way.

"It could also be wonderful timing," he countered as though he was arguing with himself.

"Papa Creola did call Sophia to him and asked me to stay back," Lunis muttered and ran his eyes over the card again. "He knows things before they happen and probably thought I could use a vacation while Soph does his bidding."

The blue dragon got to his feet and shook his tail. "Or it could be a trick," he repeated. "I mean, how did this Ward family get this card to me here? That seems like the work of a strange and mysterious being…"

Lunis knew one thing with absolute certainty: there would be no vacation at this Hotel Laguna Maldita. The invitation was a lure to get him there. It might be a trick. It could be an elaborate plan concocted by the Father of Time or another powerful creature.

He also knew something else: he wouldn't pass up the chance to learn more about his mysterious summons to Tortugas Locas.

The majestic blue dragon set off for the cave entrance without packing anything. The flight to Mexico from Scotland would be long without portal magic. Thankfully he was up for the trek across the Atlantic Ocean, his curiosity fueling the way.

CHAPTER FOUR

Kaiser sat in his dark office, his back to the door as he looked out the window at the Gulf of Mexico. It was night in Tortugas Locas—his favorite time of the day. That's when it was easiest to hide in the shadows and plot his revenge on those who'd crossed him.

Kaiser sighed with satisfaction as he enjoyed the view with nothing but the almost full moon shimmering on the water's surface to light the large office. It was finally time to put his plans into action.

Everything the man had worked on for over a decade had led up to this moment. Figuring out how to destroy the people in the idyllic tourist city of Tortugas Locas hadn't been difficult. The people who'd tried to ruin Kaiser long ago were dimwits. Deciding how to destroy the town itself also hadn't been too much of a challenge. The most complex part of the plan had been figuring out how to lure Kaiser's greatest enemy out of hiding.

It had all come together though. Kaiser would take down the people, the place, and the one who'd tried to ruin him with one swift plan.

He chuckled darkly to himself in the empty office. It would be so satisfying to watch the events about to unfold. He planned to do it from a very inconspicuous place but with a front-row seat to all the action.

All Kaiser had to do was wait until all the pieces were on the chessboard. Then he'd do what he did best and sneak onto the scene, taking a fake identity. Kaiser wasn't the dark man's real name. He'd been through dozens of personas since the ruin. That was why he survived—because he adapted.

His enemy thought they'd demolished him, but he'd simply changed so much that he was unrecognizable.

Looking across the waters outside his mansion in Tortugas Locas, Kaiser set his eyes on the warehouses in the harbor. That's where the mob guys he'd recruited would be meeting, reviewing the plans he'd given them. They had orders to take control of the city. They thought they'd get rich and powerful doing it. However, Kaiser knew they'd simply destroy the tourist destination's economy until it and its people were destitute.

Leveling the city that many people considered paradise involved a different strategy. Soon the scientist whom Kaiser had contracted would have a machine so dangerous that nothing would be left standing in Tortugas Locas. The best part was that Kaiser knew well enough that his greatest enemy would come to intervene. That's what he always did, sticking his nose where it didn't belong. This time, Kaiser would be ready. He'd demolish his arch-nemesis as he brought down the place and people that destroyed him.

CHAPTER FIVE

Something was askew. When Lunis had exited the Barrier at the Gullington—the invisible, protective dome that encompassed the Dragon Elite's headquarters—there was a shimmering blue portal waiting for him. At least he suspected it was waiting for him.

Many probably wouldn't have gone through the mysterious opening that could've led anywhere or more importantly, to anything. Most weren't Lunis. He knew that danger could be waiting on the other side, ready to ambush him. The portal could spit him out into the middle of an active volcano. *Or worse,* he thought. *It could trap me inside a vegan restaurant.*

Lunis was cautious when he stepped through the magical gateway, but he wasn't afraid. If someone was bold enough to lead him somewhere, either they were powerful and all-knowing, or they had a death wish.

To his relief, the portal spat him out on a white sand beach filled with cabanas and sunbathing tourists. The morning sun sparkled over the ocean. The turquoise water lapped on the shore —a gentle greeting as Lunis took in the beautiful sights around him. He let out a deep sigh that unfortunately sounded more like a growl, startling many of those relaxing on the beach around him.

A few women screamed. Some parents grabbed their children and ran for the resort in the distance. Police with automatic weapons raced over with frantic looks.

Lunis groaned. "Not the best start to a vacation."

The ocean winds ruffled his wings unexpectedly, and Lunis unfolded them as dragons did to keep from getting tangled. However, as more scared tourists ran for cover, he realized that he looked like he was threatening them.

"I'm not here to pillage and destroy," he announced in a loud voice. "I only want the hotel and my promised pampering!"

This sounded like another threat. The first police officer who arrived in front of Lunis pointed his weapon at him. "You can't have this hotel. We will fight you, demon dragon."

Lunis sighed. Evil dragons gave the others a bad name. Unfortunately, some demon dragons and riders didn't join Sophia's Rogue Riders but pillaged and picked on mortals. He was currently being confused for one.

"I don't want to fight." Lunis tried to fold his long wings, but the coastal winds made it difficult and forced him to flap them as he stood on his back legs. He looked like a dragon poised and ready to attack.

"He's simply going to take what he wants," a man nearby yelled. He picked up his folded umbrella and turned it to use the pole as a weapon.

"Oh brother, this isn't going well," Lunis muttered. "How about I take my leave? I'm guessing this isn't my hotel."

The police officers had created a barrier between the blue dragon and the hotel and guests. "No, this place is under our protection. Be off, demon dragon."

Lunis growled. "Don't confuse me with those soulless creatures. I'm good. I recycle."

"Sir," one of the police officers said to the one who appeared to be in charge. "I think this dragon ate the bad batch of shrimp that arrived in the harbor recently."

The guy nodded and lowered his gun. "Yeah, he's not right in the head."

"My head is fine," Lunis argued, totally offended. "You better watch out, or I'll turn this shrimp boat over and put it on my head."

"Why would you do that?" one of the police officers asked, confused.

"Because it's capsized." Lunis roared with laughter.

The police officers all looked at each other and shook their heads.

"Yeah, men, we don't have anything to worry about with this one," the officer in charge said. "This is a special dragon if you know what I mean. Return to your posts."

The men filed back toward the hotel, waving for the hiding tourists to return to their spots. "All is clear. Only a dragon who probably hatched too early," one of them yelled.

"I didn't hatch too early!" Lunis called. "But I don't have long to live."

This made the men pause and turn back to Lunis.

"Really? Why?" one of them asked.

"Yeah, my rider will be back soon," Lunis said and laughed at his joke. "Can someone tell me where Hotel Laguna Maldita is?"

The men all looked at each other and burst out laughing. "That's where you're heading?" the head officer asked.

"Yeah, I've been rewarded with an all-inclusive stay there," Lunis said proudly.

The men laughed again. "Maybe consider burning the place down," one of the police officers said.

"Yeah, that might be an improvement," another agreed.

Lunis scowled and considered blasting them with his fire. That would get back to Sophia, and there would be a proper grounding. Literally—she probably wouldn't allow him to fly for a while. She was so particular about not harming people as though there weren't a billion of them.

"If you're looking for Hotel Laguna Maldita, you're on the wrong side of the strip." An officer pointed opposite the ocean behind the row of hotels on the beach. "You want the lagoon side. Look for a rundown three-story hotel on the western part of the cove. There's a cabana on the roof and an infinity pool on the lawn that's way past the point of repair."

"Oh, and don't forget the Baron," another man imparted with a laugh. The others joined him.

"Cabana and infinity pool." Lunis smiled. "Sounds lovely. Well, thanks for the help, guys. Now you all should go and arrest a chef."

"Why would we do that?" one officer asked.

Lunis unfolded his wings, preparing to launch himself into the air. "Because they beat eggs and whip cream."

CHAPTER SIX

The water in the lagoon was placid compared to the unruly ocean. Lunis already believed that staying at Hotel Laguna Maldita would be much more relaxing than being on the busy ocean side of Tortugas Locas.

What did those dumb police officers know? He glided over the lagoon and spotted a three-story building on the western side. There was a cute little cabana he could easily see in the distance. It appeared to be the perfect spot for Lunis to enjoy the hotel's amenities.

He could already see himself getting a nice tan during the morning and splashing around in the infinity pool in the afternoon. Well, the other guests might not like the water wars, but they would grow to. Lunis was horrible at playing Marco Polo, though, since he was large and couldn't move quietly in the water.

However, he landed on the hotel's roof without much noise. Lunis looked around at the spot and shrugged. There were a few low patio chairs for sunbathing, a large umbrella that had seen better days, some potted plants, and some old patio furniture he could turn into a bed.

"It's not the Hilton, but I can work with this."

The sound of running footsteps made him turn toward the stairs. A moment later, a little girl of about twelve years old materialized. She had dark brown eyes and had pulled her blonde hair into a ponytail. Her mouth dropped open, and she pointed at him in utter shock.

"Y-Yo-You're a dragon…" the kid stuttered.

Lunis pointed at her, feigning shock. He always liked it when children spotted him because their reactions were pure. "You're a little girl!"

"Oh, my God." The child stepped forward, then took two steps backward. "Are you going to eat me?"

"No." Lunis feigned offense. "I can't stand American food. You're American, right? Based on your accent, I'm guessing you are."

"Yes, I'm American." She didn't look relieved by the admission that the huge blue dragon wouldn't eat her based on her ethnicity.

"Now if you were Italian or French, well, then I might eat you," Lunis stated.

"What are you doing here?" The girl's confidence grew. "Do you live here? Did we buy a hotel with a dragon? Do I own you now?"

Lunis gave her a confused look. "No, no one can own me, but don't tell my rider, Sophia, that. No, I live in Beverly Hills—"

"That's an odd place for a dragon to live," she interrupted.

"Well, I split my time with our summer castle in Scotland," Lunis explained. "No, I'm vacationing here because I got this." He presented the embossed piece of stationary. The girl was hesitant to approach him and take the note, although she did.

Her eyes ran over the fancy print before reading aloud,

"Lunis, you are cordially invited to enjoy a week at the all-inclusive Hotel Laguna Maldita in beautiful Tortugas Locas. Due to your service with the Dragon Elite and Rogue Riders, the Ward family would like to

pamper you to ensure you can continue to protect our globe. Please find your accommodations on the rooftop of the hotel. Meals will be available around the clock, and all your needs and expectations met. We hope you enjoy your stay."

She glanced up after reading the card, complete confusion on her face. "You're Lunis?"

"That I am," he answered proudly. "I'm excited to meet the Ward family who will be pampering me and honoring my service to the planet."

"I'm Laura Ward, but my family didn't send this."

Lunis lowered his chin. Smoke issued from his nostrils. "Say what?"

"Yeah, my mother and father, well, they're struggling to keep the hotel going. So they wouldn't have sent this. Although we've heard dragons are real, we didn't believe it. I didn't until now. So there's no way my father would've sent this to you. Or even known where to send it."

"So this *is* a trap," Lunis muttered, confirming what he'd thought since the beginning but not deterred. "No wonder there are no pillows or high thread-count comforters up here. Can we change that?"

"You said it was a trap." Laura suddenly looked around. "Why would you stay?"

"Well, because if someone lured me here, I want to meet this guy and he can meet my flame. Also, my rider Sophia is off on a solo mission or something. Therefore I have some spare time to kill...not you. I won't kill you...probably...maybe...most likely not."

Laura giggled, obviously entertained by his antics. "So you're staying?"

"Are you getting me pillows and meals around the clock?"

"Well, I don't know." Laura deflated. "I might get in trouble. Maybe if my parents know—"

"You can't tell your parents," Lunis interrupted.

"I can't lie to them."

"No, you can't. But something is awry here. I've been brought here for a reason and the fewer who know about me, the better."

"Well, what if my dad comes up here and finds you? I mean, no one ever comes up here, but what if he does?"

"So if no one comes up here, why did you?" Lunis followed the clues.

"Oh, I saw this strange cat and followed him," Laura said at once and looked around. "I don't know where he went."

"A cat, you say…" Lunis gazed around the rooftop, looking for Plato the lynx. He should've known he was behind this. This was all starting to make sense. The invitation, the portal, this unfolding mission. Yes, Lunis was probably going to stay at this point, depending on how Laura answered his next question. "Was this cat black and white, perchance?"

"He was!" Laura exclaimed.

"Nice work, Plato," Lunis sang, narrowing his eyes and looking around the patio rooftop but not finding the sneaky feline. "So what is it you want me to do?"

"Say what?" Laura asked.

The blue dragon redirected his attention to the young girl. "You said your family is struggling to keep the hotel open." Lunis settled down on the rooftop, getting comfortable. "Tell me more, Laura Ward. Tell me all the pertinent details."

"Oh, well, we just bought this place," Laura explained. "My mother is from Mexico and a great chef. My dad has always dreamed of owning and operating a small hotel. So they jumped on this opportunity."

"But you don't like it here." Lunis picked up on the regret in her tone.

"Well, I don't have any friends here."

Lunis nodded. "But your mother is from Mexico, so this means a lot to her."

"Yeah, I guess." Laura kicked the rooftop.

"Hey, do you know what you call a Mexican with a rubber toe?" Lunis suddenly looked serious.

Laura glanced up, confused. "What? Huh?"

"Roberto!"

The young girl blinked at him. "Was that a joke?"

Lunis huffed. "If this is going to work, you have to know when I'm telling a joke."

"If what's going to work?"

"Me swooping in and saving the hotel from whatever it needs saving from," Lunis stated.

Laura shrugged. "I don't know. I mean, we don't really have any customers, well, except those mean guys who bullied Dad earlier."

Lunis paused her, holding up a single talon like a finger. "Back up. Tell me about these guys."

"Oh, well, Dad called them mobsters or something. They aren't going to pay for rooms and threatened him. I don't know…"

"Keep going," Lunis urged.

"Well, then there's the weird noises the boiler makes. It makes it difficult to sleep at night. Mom thinks something's haunting the hotel. Dad says that she's exhausted and sleep-deprived. Anyway, the noise should be gone soon because a scientist showed up today. She's staying at the hotel and offered to fix the boiler for us."

"Interesting," Lunis mused.

"Is it?" Laura asked. "I don't know. I think we should move back and give up this dream of living in Mexico."

"Yeah, maybe." Lunis suddenly looked up. "Oh, hey. That reminds me. Do you know why the Mexican couldn't practice archery?"

Confusion resurfaced on Laura's face. "What?"

"Because he didn't habanero." Lunis laughed at his joke.

Laura caught the punch line and let out an easy laugh. "Oh,

that was funny."

"Of course it was," he said coolly. "Oh, did you hear about the Mexican train killer? He had a locomotive."

Laura laughed harder. "You're really funny. I can't believe I met a dragon *and* he tells jokes."

"Awesome jokes," Lunis added.

"So you're going to stay?" Laura asked.

"Are you going to feed me?"

"Will you tell me awesome jokes?"

"You couldn't stop me even if you wanted to," he stated. "Believe me. Many have tried and failed."

"You think there's something here you need to save us from?" Laura cautiously looked around.

"It sounds like there's a lot of suspicious activity," Lunis answered. "If Plato set this up, well, it's probably one of the most important missions I'll attend to this year."

"Then maybe I can find you something soft to sleep on." Laura pointed at where he was lying on tattered patio cushions.

"I prefer bamboo sheets and organic down comforters," he supplied.

She scrunched up her nose. "I might be able to get some light blankets from one of the unused rooms."

"Deal," Lunis chirped.

"How about I go and get you something from the kitchen to eat? I think Mom made some extra roast beef since we have more guests tonight."

"I think this is going to be the start of a beautiful partnership."

"Me too." The young girl headed for the stairs and retreated at once.

With such stunning views of the lagoon, most looked at the water rather than up at the roof. So no one spied Lunis as he watched the grounds of Hotel Laguna Maldita. If anyone glanced up, the blue dragon was smart enough that he'd glamoured himself to look like something ordinary to undiscerning eyes.

The mobsters whom Laura had told Lunis about weren't discerning. They were downright selfish, rude, and loud. From his place on the rooftop, Lunis had watched as the three men bossed the Ward family and the hotel staff around.

The boss, apparently a man by the name of Donte, thought the new waiter was his servant. He yelled at Emmanuel to get him more drinks on a regular basis.

The other two goons weren't bright enough to mastermind any real trouble. However, they were sloppy and created messes everywhere they went. Plus, they were inconsiderate and bullies, two things Lunis couldn't stand.

The mob guys were part of the problem he was here to fix. However, that wasn't enough, and the blue dragon knew it. Another piece of the equation was why the mysterious lynx had summoned him. Plato played with big problems, so Lunis needed time to figure out what the lynx intended for him to do.

The night before hadn't offered the luxurious sleep Lunis had been after. Although Laura had brought him some pillows, blankets, and a nice meal, he'd still slept fretfully. Lunis didn't think that was because of the balmy temperatures. Dragons liked warm weather. Really, they were fine with any weather.

It wasn't even the noise from the hotel bar that had been a problem. A strange rumbling underneath the blue dragon kept jerking him away from sleep. He thought it might be old pipes or something, but his intuition told him otherwise.

Something wasn't right about Hotel Laguna Maldita. Lunis' job was to figure it out. He suspected it would be a lot more complex than he'd bargained for. Although Lunis was up for the challenge, he wasn't used to working alone and silently wished he had a friend to help him on this case.

CHAPTER EIGHT

When the sun was high in the Mexican sky, Lunis was awoken from a lazy afternoon nap by the sounds of scratching claws on the hotel's exterior. He stirred in time to throw glamour up to camouflage himself as two large eyes peeked up over the side of the rooftop.

A moment later, a little squirrel Lunis had known for quite some time and liked a lot stood on the edge of the hotel. The intelligent creature held a small, strange lens to one of his eyes and peered through it in his direction before snickering. "As I suspected... You can take down your glamour, Lunis. I see you."

The small rodent must've suspected the blue dragon was using glamour to hide in case one of the guests or employees came up to the roof.

Realizing the squirrel had caught him, Lunis dropped the glamour and materialized at once with a wide grin.

"Well, hey there, Faraday. Did you win an all-inclusive vacation to this place too?"

The squirrel shook his head, climbed over the ledge, and scurried closer to the dragon. The pair had worked together on other missions and as Beaufonts, knew each other quite well.

"No, I received an internship to learn Mexican cooking. Surprisingly, I didn't apply for the opportunity. How about you?"

"Yeah, it was like the package dropped magically into my lap." Lunis sniffed the air. "Do you smell a rat?"

"More like a feline." Faraday snickered.

"How did you know I was up here?"

"Well, although Laura is growing, I didn't buy that the twelve-year-old ate an entire rack of lamb. That's what she tried to convince her mother of when it went missing."

Lunis licked his chops. "That rack of lamb was delicious."

"Then I put together that someone had lured me here. I believe it was Plato," Faraday continued.

The blue dragon nodded. "Oh, yes, this whole situation reeks of the magical lynx."

"I figured that if Plato lured me here to solve the goings-on, he might've also secretly recruited you."

"Yes, dear Watson, I think your observation is accurate."

Faraday grimaced and crossed his tiny arms. "Why do you get to be Sherlock Holmes in this scenario?"

"Isn't it obvious?"

"Not really," Faraday said grumpily.

"Because I smoke a pipe." Lunis held an imaginary pipe to his mouth and blew out smoke rings.

The squirrel laughed. "That's the other way I figured you out. Francesca said she kept smelling a bonfire when tidying up the lawn area and hearing a flapping sound."

"Hey, you didn't expect me to eat the rack of lamb raw. I'm a dragon, not a savage."

Faraday nodded. "So you smoked it. That makes sense."

"I have a related question for you." Lunis hid a grin.

"I'm certain you don't," the squirrel replied dryly.

"If we are what we eat, does that make you nuts?"

Faraday didn't laugh. Instead, he shook his head. "I saw that joke coming a mile away. You know I'm allergic to nuts."

"Right, because that's not weird for a squirrel."

"I talk," Faraday countered. "That's what makes me weird."

"Plus that whole science thing you do." Lunis indicated the monocle hanging from Faraday's neck.

"Yes, and I've deduced that my science background is one of the reasons Plato enlisted my help," Faraday explained. "I discovered a nutty magitech scientist stripping the boiler of essential parts. From what I've observed, she's trying to create a machine that generates a hurricane."

Lunis looked up at the brooding storm clouds overhead. "Looks like she might be succeeding. Did you recognize the machine she's working on? Is that how you know she intends to create a hurricane?"

Faraday shook his head. "No, the nutter talks to herself incessantly. She pretty much disclosed that some man hired her to build the machine. Doctor Beth Hailey doesn't plan to create the full hurricane, but her testing has created a potential storm. I suspect it will only get worse."

Lunis huffed. "Oh, great. Maybe I can get a room inside the hotel."

"I doubt it. That's the other problem brewing in the hotel. Have you heard about the mobsters who have taken over in there?"

"Yeah, Laura told me about them."

Faraday nodded. "Yeah, their wrath is getting worse, and the family is suffering. They intimidate all the guests and make a lot of unreasonable demands."

"The greedy little jerks need to be taught a lesson."

Faraday flicked his tail. "I agree. Then, on top of that, I think a ghost is haunting the hotel. Jack thinks the malfunctioning boiler is the cause of the incessant knocking noises in the walls. However, the boiler didn't have any problems until Dr. Hailey started stripping parts from it. As Francesca said, I've noticed objects fly off shelves and the exterior walls shaking."

"Which wouldn't be the case if it were a boiler issue," Lunis mused, combing his claws over his chin like a detective thinking about a case.

"Yes, so I thought maybe we could do some research on Hotel Laguna Maldita," Faraday began. "The family doesn't know anything about the place. Neither one of us can quiz the locals to get information."

"Because talking squirrels and dragons freak mortals out," Lunis cut in.

"Exactly," Faraday chirped. "So I can take a trip to the Great Library and see if Paul, the Great Librarian, can help me find history on this place. If someone recorded it, then it would be there."

Lunis gauged the dark clouds overhead again. "You better hurry on that one because something tells me that we don't have long."

Suddenly, an old leather-bound book appeared beside the two magical creatures, followed by a *popping* sound. They both swung around, looking alert. Their eyes darted to the book sitting on the rooftop.

Faraday arched an eyebrow at Lunis. "That book wasn't there a moment ago, was it?"

"I don't believe so, dear Watson."

"Again, why do you get to be Sherlock?" Faraday complained. "You tell too many bad jokes to be the great detective."

"Just for that, I'm not entertaining you with any of my jokes, and you pronounced awesome wrong."

Lunis made his way over to the book in one step while Faraday scurried in several hops. The blue dragon leaned over the tome, flipping to a marked page. His eyes widened at once. "Watson. Come at once if convenient. If inconvenient, come all the same."

Faraday hurried around to the other side of the book, which the large blue dragon mostly blocked. It appeared to be a history of Tortugas Locas. "So you've given up jokes to quote Sherlock Holmes now? How do you know those?"

Lunis looked up from the book and winked. "My name is Sherlock Holmes. It is my business to know what other people don't know."

Faraday laughed. "Wow, I set you up perfectly for that."

Lunis tapped the book with his claw. "Look at this. It's the history of Hotel Laguna Maldita."

Faraday's gaze scanned the words as he muttered, "Built in… duh…duh…duh…" He skipped down several passages. "The ownership traded hands several times…duh…duh…duh…"

"Wow, take a speed-reading class." Lunis laughed and pointed at the bottom of the page with his sharp claw. "Down here is the story of our ghost, I believe." He cleared his throat and began to read from the book.

"A baron by the name of Fabien Coulter stole his family's fortune, enraging his six older brothers. Fabien escaped to Tortugas Locas to 'live like a king' and elude being hunted down by his siblings. He moved into Hotel Laguna Maldita and lived a lavish lifestyle with dozens of servants, famous guests, and rich foods.

"However, it didn't last for long. The Coulter brothers tracked him down, retrieved the stolen riches, locked him in his hotel, surrounded it, and declared that if he tried to leave, one of the brothers would kill him on the spot. Left with nothing but his hotel and bare rations, Fabien Coulter lasted ten days before taking his life."

Faraday's chin jerked up, his eyes wide. "It's the baron who haunts the hotel. That makes perfect sense."

"It appears that this saved you the time and trouble of going to the Great Library for research."

"Yes, thanks, Plato," Faraday called over his shoulder.

Lunis snickered. "In truth, I think the one playing the real Sherlock Holmes is that magical lynx."

"I suspect you're correct," Faraday mused. "So we have a mad scientist creating a hurricane, a boiler that's about to blow, three mobsters creating trouble, and an angry ghost. I see why Plato recruited our help, but how do you suppose he expects us to fix all these problems?"

"There is nothing more deceptive than an obvious fact." Lunis pretended to smoke a pipe again.

"Would you stop quoting Sherlock Holmes and say what you mean?" Faraday insisted.

"We could take down each of our three villains," Lunis began. "I'm confident that we could. Or we could use them to take each other down."

Faraday gasped. "Yes! Of course, that would be a Plato strategy. Why fight your enemies when you can make them fight each other."

"Elementary, my dear Watson." Lunis winked at the squirrel.

Faraday tapped his paw against his chin while thinking. "Okay, I think I have a plan that could pen our villains together and get rid of them before they create too much trouble."

Lunis leaned close. "Okay, I'm ready to hear your plan and take full credit for its brilliance."

"So you're telling me that this storm isn't real?" Laura wrapped her arms around her torso in a futile attempt to protect herself from the wind and rain.

Lunis extended his wing and propped it over the young girl who'd dared to climb up here to see him as the hurricane built all around the lagoon. "Well, the winds and all are real enough. It's what produced them that isn't real. However, my friend and I are on the case. We're going to get to the bottom of things and end this."

"What about the mob guys?"

"We have a plan for them." He smiled down at her and noticed she was shivering from the cold. "You should get inside."

"I'm fine," she insisted. "I want to know what's going on."

"You do. You know what you have to do."

"That doesn't seem very important," she argued. "I want a real job."

"Sometimes the biggest jobs are the ones we think aren't important, but they lay the framework for the battles."

She looked up at him. "So telling the mobsters about the diamonds arriving on the boat in the harbor is a big deal?"

"It's part of it." He and Faraday thought they could take the mobsters down if they lured them from the hotel. They'd concocted a story that the storm had forced a boat full of diamonds to dock in the harbor. The thieves couldn't resist sitting treasure. That was part of the equation. "Remember the other part. It's equally important."

"You want me to talk to myself?"

Lunis shook his head. "No, you're talking to someone, even if you can't see them."

She shivered harder. This time not because of the rain, but rather from fear. "There's really a ghost in our hotel…"

"Well, there won't be for long," Lunis reasoned. "But you're going to have to lay the framework, which means pitting him against our opponents. You can do it."

"You said that like a statement." Doubt lay heavy in her eyes.

"Because it is," he stated with confidence. "You have to believe it and make it happen. Then another piece will be set in motion."

"You'll sweep in and fight the battle?" Laura asked.

He nodded. "Help me get all the pieces on the chessboard, and I'll checkmate our opponents."

CHAPTER TEN

" an you hear me?" Laura's voice crackled over the walkie-talkie.

Lunis grinned and pressed the button on the side of his unit. "Copy, Little Player. Over and out."

She giggled.

He knew the young soccer player was brave. Still, he was asking her to do a lot. She was about to have a conversation for a ghost's benefit to set the stage. So he did something he'd offered Sophia many times and gave Laura the illusion of support. She would be alone inside the haunted hotel, leaking information. However, the walkie-talkie would make her feel like she wasn't.

Usually, Lunis talked to Sophia in her head, and she answered him out loud for situations like this. Since Laura and he weren't telepathically linked, the walkie-talkies were the best option. It would also seem more realistic to the ghost.

"I'm almost there," Laura murmured.

Lunis knew by "there" she meant the boiler room where Baron Fabien Coulter's ghost was most active. The timing had to be perfect, so Laura had waited until Doctor Beth Hailey had gone to grab a cup of tea, something she did reliably after several hours of work.

"The walls are shaking," Laura muttered.

"It's only the storm," Lunis lied. Although the hurricane was building, he was on the rooftop and knew that if the walls were shaking, it was most likely from a force within Hotel Laguna Maldita. It was probably the ghost, but he needed Laura to be brave. He knew she was.

"There's a weird howling noise," she transmitted.

"It's from the boiler. Do you see the machinery yet?"

"I'm almost there." Her rehearsed reply was right on schedule. "You're telling me that Dr. Beth Hailey is trying to destroy the hotel with the device she created?"

"I am." He followed the script. The ghost was listening at this point. Lunis knew that because the howling softened over the walkie-talkie as Laura spoke.

"I don't get it, though." Laura sounded confused. The girl was a good actress. "Why does she want to destroy our hotel?"

"Because the Coulter family's descendants hired her." Lunis followed his script. "They learned that Fabien's ghost resides in here. They won't rest until they've destroyed him and the place he once called home."

The howling suddenly grew so loud that Lunis tensed. He stood, ready to fly down to the first floor if needed. His heart raced as he worried that he'd put Laura in danger.

A moment later, her voice came through the speaker. "I think the storm has picked up."

He sighed. The winds hadn't changed on the rooftop, but it sounded as though the ghost had gotten the message. "Well, we're not going to allow Dr. Beth Hailey to harm the hotel, are we, Laura? We're on the side of good, aren't we?"

"That's right."

Lunis heard the smile in her voice despite all the howling in the background.

"Good people have to stop bad people, don't they?" Lunis continued.

"Yes, but I'm not sure how I can."

"I'm not certain either. I only wish there was a way to scare her from this hotel. Then her work would be over and the machine no longer able to do damage."

"I'm only a little girl." Laura suddenly sounded nervous. It was a scripted reaction, but Lunis didn't think she had to act for it to be convincing.

"Yeah, maybe we're in over our heads."

"Plus, I have homework to do," Laura added.

"Okay, we'll think about this. Why don't you go work on your homework in the lobby for now?"

"Sounds good," she agreed in a rush, hardly audible over the howling around her. "I want to tell Emmanuel about the diamond boat harbored here."

"Good idea." Lunis smiled, realizing that the least suspect player was putting everything in place on the chessboard.

CHAPTER ELEVEN

The hurricane machine was doing what Dr. Hailey intended and creating a storm unlike anything else that had battered Tortugas Locas. However, the blue dragon stood firmly on the rooftop of Hotel Laguna Maldita, looking down at the lawn. Dragons were built to withstand storms, wind, and harsh elements.

Lunis watched with focused intensity as the mad scientist ran from the first story below, right after screaming louder than the piercing wind. Her continuing cries were audible over a deep voice that chanted, "You dare to terrorize my home?"

The crazy woman trembled as she stood on the lawn and regarded the hotel she'd escaped from. She was visibly weighing her options. Behind her was the lagoon with its storm-tossed waves. Where she'd come from was something that filled her with more dread.

When the ghostly voice screamed, it made up her mind.

Dr. Beth Hailey spun at once, dove into the choppy waters, and quickly disappeared in the storm haze. Lunis didn't worry about her. His only concern was whether the little squirrel who knew magitech better than most could reverse the machine in the boiler room.

If he could, the device would become something to take care of the ghost, now that they'd frightened away the mad scientist. Lunis was hopeful that their plan to pit their enemies against each other would work because those with evil motivations were easy to manipulate.

He peered over the edge of the hotel and watched for signs of the next villains—he'd deal with them directly.

CHAPTER TWELVE

R ight on schedule, Lunis watched as the three goons
headed out to the jet boat. Only those fueled by fear or
greed would venture out in a storm of this magnitude. These
men wanted treasure, but they would never reach their
destination.

After a quick exchange, the men turned the boat out toward
the turbulent sea and raced toward the harbor on the lagoon's far
side. Lunis gave them a small head start and sprang off the Hotel
Laguna Maldita's roof, his blue wings flapping effortlessly in the
gusty winds.

It would be hard to spot Lunis in the storm's dense spray. The
mobsters weren't looking over their shoulders anyway. They
were so intent on reaching their destination and robbing the boat
of its diamonds that their attention was all directed forward.
That made Lunis' surprise entrance even more satisfying.

Lunis easily caught up with the jet boat and zoomed ahead of
it, darting through the torrential winds and sheets of rain. Flying
in the worst conditions was nothing for him. However, the small
boat below in the choppy waters couldn't handle storms of this
magnitude for long. Most things couldn't.

Lunis knew why dragons were so unstoppable. It was because the good ones were there to protect—to bring justice to the world. Sometimes that meant doing the hard jobs.

He overtook the boat speeding through the whitecapped lagoon and dove without hesitating. He then did the one thing he knew would put a bone-chilling fear into the mobsters.

Lunis stopped and froze in mid-air right in front of the boat, his wings only beating enough to keep him aloft.

At that short distance, he saw the whites of the men's eyes as they registered what was happening. A prehistoric dragon had materialized out of nowhere and was playing chicken with them in a hurricane.

Donte jerked the wheel to the side, nearly making the boat capsize. Lunis shook his head. He had to hand it to the greedy mobster. He was willing to do whatever it took to get to his treasure. The goons could've turned back, but instead, they pulled weapons and started firing at Lunis.

"Well, this got good," Lunis said. "Now I have to fire back."

The blue dragon opened his mouth and blasted fire, sending it straight at the jet boat.

Unfortunately, a waterspout so powerful that it pulled Lunis out of his hover formed at that exact moment. The jet boat rose from the water too, getting air before dropping at the base of a massive wave. It powered up the large arch, and Lunis panicked, unable to do anything momentarily.

He was frantic, worried that the goons would crest the wave and make it to safety before he could get to them. The waterspout kept him powerless in its grip. His wings didn't work. Shooting fire was useless when he was so far from the boat speeding away. His attempts to fight the wind were futile.

Then he remembered something his rider had once told him. "When we resist the wind, we make our jobs harder. When we embrace it, we coast along with it."

Lunis stopped fighting the funnel. He stopped panicking. He

pretended Sophia was on his back and he was one with his rider. She always made him stronger. She always made him content in the face of battle. He'd almost lost that. Now he remembered that even if Sophia wasn't with him, her spirit was.

As quickly as he'd lost his focus, Lunis regained it. Suddenly he was gliding on the wind created by the crazy weather phenomenon. Instead of taking him away from the jet boat, it sent him in that direction faster than ever.

The blue dragon dove for the jet boat full of criminals like a bullet. He wouldn't let them reach the harbor in the distance. Once more, Lunis opened his mouth and sent a roiling blast of fire at the jet boat. The rain and wind didn't shield it this time, and the dragon's fire hit the fuel tank. The explosion launched the three men into the choppy seas. The fiery blast was visible for miles.

Lunis veered to the east in a sharp turn, shielding himself from the blast and quickly flapping his wings to recover from the spray of fire, water, and wind. His friends back at Hotel Laguna Maldita would see the explosion. They'd know he stopped the mobsters and hopefully taught them a lesson.

He had every hope that Faraday would be equally successful at trapping the baron and saving the hotel from the villain who had terrorized it for so long.

CHAPTER THIRTEEN

"So that's what happened on my end." Lunis looked around at the aftermath of the battles they'd waged at Hotel Laguna Maldita. He'd finished telling Plato and Faraday his part of the story.

He looked over his shoulder at the Ward family and smiled at the brave little girl, feeling a unique fondness for her. Laura waved and smiled from the table with her family. Her brown eyes held a grateful look.

"Wow, you were so brave, going after those goons," Faraday stated. "They're gone?"

"That they are," Plato stated casually. "They've set sail for new lives that won't cause trouble."

Lunis snickered. "I hoped I'd scare them straight."

"And Dr. Beth Hailey?" Faraday asked.

"She washed up on the shore next to the airport," Plato explained. "She doesn't remember anything and won't create dangerous magitech any longer."

"Your next bottle of whiskey." Emmanuel the waiter set another bottle of Glenlivet on the table.

Plato glanced at the waiter. He didn't say a word, but his

expression conveyed, "Good, now be off." When the waiter was gone, he turned his attention back to his companions. "The Baron?"

"Well, you know that I got rid of him," Faraday chirped.

"Yes, but we don't know how," Lunis stated. "I know Plato's side of the story, masterminding everything. I know my side, looking awesome and telling fantastic jokes. I don't know yours entirely. I want to know how you rid Hotel Laguna Maldita of that ghoul and how exactly you came to be here."

Faraday sipped his whiskey and nodded. "Okay, well, I'll tell you my tale. It all started three days ago…"

Lunis grinned and leaned forward, but his eyes still scanned the hotel. He couldn't wait to hear the story about to be told. He also couldn't wait for the next adventure with his friends. There was nothing better than making the world a better place.

Well, there was, and it was making the world a better place alongside those you cherished dearly. Friends made everything better. They made the world worth saving over and over again.

Something Lunis would do until the end of time.

A huge thank you to all of you for reading our books, these short stories and putting up with my author notes. Thank you to all of the readers and the LMBPN team.

Oh Lunis, the antithesis of most majestic dragons. I have so much to say about this dragon. Let me start at the beginning…

You all heard MA groan, didn't you?

Anyway, back to my story…

When I first began the Exceptional S. Beaufont series starting with Sophia and Lunis, I wanted to do something new. I had read a few dragon books and I knew how they were depicted. Most were stuffy and all-knowing and all up-tight and regal. And I was like, no, no no. "How about we have a young blue dragon who tells bad jokes and eats Doritos and spends too much money on phone app upgrades?" And poof, the magical Lunis was born.

Since the S. Beaufont series, I've gone on to write the Paris Beaufont series. However, when I bring Lunis back, it is easy words. Because that dragon writes his own scenes. I just let him on the page, he tells some bad jokes, flies over and saves the day and there you go.

What I love is that you all didn't mind that I didn't go with the traditional dragon. I worried. Really worried. I was like, they are going to expect the dragon to spout wisdom and not knock-knock jokes. They will want him to know history rather than the easiest way to drown a blonde. The readers will expect combat flying rather than info on the latest Netflix comedy. And yet, you all seemed to like Lunis. Actually when polled you all seemed to like the blue dragon more than the humans. And what's not to like? He's pretty lovable. If there's anyone I want by my side in battle, it's the reptile who breathes fire and can crack my ribs with laughter.

Incidentally, I told a few of the Lunis' jokes over Thanksgiving dinner this year and my friends just stared at me like I'd lost my mind. Seriously weirdos, what's not to laugh about? The last time I drank juice, I lost two hours of my life…because the bottle said, "concentrate."

If you're not laughing then Lunis is coming after you!

Much love and Peace,
Tiny Ninja

MICHAEL'S AUTHOR NOTES

WRITTEN DECEMBER 12, 2021

Thank you for not only reading this book but these author notes as well!

I'm in Las Vegas at the moment, and the weather has finally gotten cold. Here in the desert, it just about hit freezing (0 Celsius) last night.

I have more than a handful of Dragon books with other collaborators, but only one dragon-based book as a second-level (not even FIRST!) character where I'm the main one involved.

The series is appropriately titled "Myth of the Dragon" and is actually a Fantasy book, not an Urban Fantasy book.

Wivre is a small dragon, fairly old but very malnourished. So, he has all the snark of a dragon but can't snap up his food and eat those he finds annoying.

In short, not having so much fun being a dragon...yet. He is now on a better eating regimen, and I hope that after a few books, we shall see a larger reptile.

I've always enjoyed dragon characters, and when Sarah and I started working on the covers of this series, it was fun trying to come up with poses for a dragon that (perhaps) stretched what a dragon-on-your-cover might look like.

My favorite is Linus in his large form with a jumbo jet on the cover in *Chi of the Dragon (The Exceptional Sophia Beaufont Book 05)*. I kept chuckling, thinking about this cover as if the co-pilot all of a sudden looks up and sees this massive dragon above him. Finally, he stammers a request for the pilot to look up. The pilot gives him crap.

Until HE sees the dragon.

I am not doing the scene justice in my head, but it tickles my funny bone. If you would like to see the cover,

Have a great weekend, or week, and talk to you in the next book!

Ad Aeternitatem,

Michael Anderle

THE PHENOMENAL FARADAY

A BEAUFONT SHORT STORY BOOK 3

CHAPTER ONE

Most who occupied the lobby of Hotel Laguna Maldita thought the dangers were over. Faraday and his companions knew better.

The real battle had just begun.

Sitting around the bar table in the corner, Faraday, the talking squirrel, flicked his tail, his eyes skittering between the lynx and the dragon across from him. Lunis had just finished telling his side of the story, recounting what he'd been doing the last three days to stop the villains from attacking the coastal city of Tortugas Locas. Before him, Plato had indulged them, explaining what Faraday had already guessed—that the black and white cat had orchestrated many of the events that had brought the squirrel and dragon to Mexico.

Soon it would be time for Faraday to tell his story, but he wasn't quick to dive into his tale. His small brown eyes scanned the hotel lobby, which lay in chaos.

The large wrought iron chandelier that hung in the middle was still intact, but many of the candles had been knocked out. Cracks in the plaster and broken paintings on the walls were reminders of the battle waged inside Hotel Laguna Maldita. The floor-to-ceiling windows that had showcased the now-placid lagoon were shattered reminders of the battle that had happened outside. Coconuts and debris were strewn across the lawn, signs of the storm that had just passed.

Faraday's gaze ran over the destruction and the hotel guests and even the Ward family, who were celebrating the passing of the many storms. The squirrel was only interested in watching one person—the one he believed was the villain behind everything that had happened. It wasn't time to confront them yet, though. That moment was approaching soon, but first, the final and third side of the story had to be told—Faraday's.

"Your next bottle of whisky," Emmanuel, the waiter, said, setting another bottle of Glenlivet on the table.

Plato just cut his eyes to the waiter, not saying a word. His expression made his thoughts clear: "Good, now be off." When the waiter was gone, he turned his attention back to his companions. "And the baron?" the lynx asked, referring to the ghost who had been haunting Hotel Laguna Maldita.

"Well, you know I got rid of him," Faraday chirped, hiding his pride at his accomplishment. Trapping the ghost of Baron Fabien Coulter hadn't been easy; it had been a stroke of genius mixed with fortuitous coincidence. The talking squirrel who had more than one advanced degree in science didn't believe in coincidence, though, or not in the way that most thought of it. Coincidence wasn't luck but rather a confluence of events drawn together by cosmic forces.

"Yes, but we don't know how," Lunis stated, the blue dragon blinking at Faraday from across the table. "I know Plato's side of the story; he masterminded everything. I know my side; I looked awesome and told fantastic jokes. But I don't know yours. I want to know how you rid this hotel of that ghoul and how you came to be here."

Faraday took a sip of his whisky and nodded. "Okay, well, I'll tell you my tale. It all started three days ago…"

CHAPTER TWO

Three Days Previous...

Paris Beaufont sighed and lowered her phone, her brow furrowed. "I thought a chimichanga was like a parka."

Faraday shook his head. He was on the counter bar in the restaurant. Little Pleasures, a farm-to-table café, was closed. Out in the field, vegetables were being harvested, and the animals were attended to in the barn. In the kitchen, Clark Beaufont, the head chef of the organic restaurant, was whistling as he prepped for that night's dinner service. It would be another busy night, with a packed house and excited patrons.

However, the most recent customer review on Yelp.com was occupying Paris' attention rather than the prospect of many satisfied diners coming that evening. Faraday, sensing that he could steer things in a more positive direction, flicked his tail and regarded her thoughtfully.

"It's just one review," he countered. "Look at all the other glowing ones that rave about the food and the service."

Paris glanced out the long bank of windows at the green mountains of Colorado in the distance, not really seeing them.

"That's not the way to improve. This reviewer says we don't do Mexican food right. The spices are off, and the construction is not authentic." She recited the last part from memory, having read the critical review a dozen times.

"Then we simply take the Mexican items off the menu."

Again, she sighed. "I can't. You know what my mother's favorite food is."

He nodded. "Nachos. I think everyone knows. She talks about them incessantly."

"And the whole idea of Little Pleasures is to deliver just that—small comforts," Paris continued. "And one key to that is to offer a wide variety of comfort foods so we have something for everyone. We have all the major cuisines—American, Asian, Italian, but our Mexican is lacking."

"Well, I'm actually surprised since your Uncle Clark grew up in Los Angeles," Faraday stated. "You'd think he'd have a better handle on what goes into an enchilada."

Paris agreed with a discreet smirk. "My uncle isn't really the type to hang out at a taco truck. I think his culinary talents are considered a bit more refined, which is nice but means we're missing an opportunity. People love their chips and salsa."

"It is the simple things in life that are the most rewarding," Faraday imparted.

Paris held up her phone, indicating the Yelp review. "Yeah, and this patron didn't want a shaved butternut squash burrito with truffle oil and aged cheese."

The talking squirrel snickered. "No, apparently, they wanted a soaked chimichanga with refried beans covered in cheddar."

Paris groaned with frustration. "I can't blame them. That sounds amazing and more pleasant than some froufrou dish."

The farm-to-table restaurant, Little Pleasures, was Paris' passion project. The objective was to use magical and nonmagical ingredients and practices to make diners happy on a basic level. The food might spark a fond childhood memory, or a drink could bring about momentary euphoria. The farm's grounds and the restaurant's décor were meant to appeal to everyone in one way or another. However, Paris wasn't going to be satisfied until her menu was perfect, which meant it had to have something for everyone.

"Well, maybe Clark can take a class on Mexican cuisine," Faraday offered, always trying to find a solution.

Paris shook her head as she exchanged her phone for the stack of mail sitting on the open bar beside her. She began shuffling through the letters, most notes expressing gratitude for the experiences the restaurant offered or requests to hold a special event there. "He's already stretched to the limit with the dinner service. And I can't forget that his first responsibility is being a Councilor for the House of Fourteen, which takes up his mornings."

Faraday nodded, impressed by how Clark juggled his schedule. He was a master of discipline, though, and didn't really have a social life. He preferred to work rather than date or make friends.

"Well, maybe you can—"

"Don't even suggest that I learn how to make tacos," Paris interrupted, continuing to comb through the mail. "I've got that new case in the Arctic."

Faraday grinned. "I think it's in Canada, actually."

"Same thing," Paris stated. "I definitely don't have time to figure out what the difference is between cilantro and coriander."

"They are parts of the same thing," Faraday explained. "Those who are right call it by the first name. Those who are wrong call it by the latter."

Paris glanced up from the mail, arching an eyebrow. "Do I sense a bias?"

"My old lab partner used to say it wrong."

Tearing into a thick envelope, Paris chuckled. "Sometimes I

forget that you had a whole life as a science geek before you decided to be my sidekick."

He harrumphed. "I'm not sure which is more offensive, that you called me a geek or your sidekick. I like to think of myself as your partner."

"Not my lab partner, though," she teased.

"Well, you'd have to know something…anything about science for that to be the case."

Pulling a thick card out of the envelope, Paris shot him a mock look of offense. "I know about science. Like, I know all about physics."

He crossed his tiny arms over his furry chest. "Oh, this should be good. Go on."

"Well, like, Newton's third law of motion," she stated, hiding her grin behind the card in her hand.

"That for every action, there is an equal and opposite reaction," Faraday offered.

"Right. So, you insult me, and I'll drop-kick you, Squirrel. Which would give us a lesson on Newton's second law of motion."

Faraday rolled his eyes. "That the acceleration of an object is directly proportional to the net force applied and inversely proportional to the mass of an object."

She winked at him. "Bingo."

"Your threats don't scare me."

Paris' eyes ran over the card in her hand, her expression morphing into one of disbelief. "Well, if that doesn't, this might."

Faraday rose on his back legs. "What's that?"

She turned the card around, flashing it in his direction. "It is, strangely enough, an invitation for you to learn Mexican cuisine from a world-renowned chef. What are the odds?"

Faraday gulped as he hurried over to Paris to get a better look at the card, which was filled with print. "I estimate that the odds are zero, which leads me to hypothesize that this is a trick."

"Why do you have to be so cynical?" Paris asked, handing Faraday the note. "This sounds like a wonderful invitation, although the timing is a little coincidental."

"There is no such thing as coincidence," Faraday remarked, grabbing the card with his paws. It was bigger than him.

"Of course there is. Just ask Stephen Hawking," Paris fired back.

Unable to resist, Faraday peered at her instead of reading the note in his paws. "I don't have to explain why that's impossible, do I?"

"Because he's dead," she answered proudly. "And did you know that Hawking was born on the three-hundredth anniversary of Galileo's death and died on Einstein's birthday?"

Faraday's eyes bulged in surprise. "I'm a little shocked that you know those pieces of information."

She stuck her chin higher in the air. "I know things. And there you go; those are coincidences. They *do* exist."

Still unable to pull his attention away from this strange yet typical conversation with Paris, he kept his eyes off the card that was begging for his focus. "Although I'll admit that the events happening on the same days based on the scientific connections between those three men is strange, statistically speaking, it isn't improbable. People are born and die every day. That's a fact. What we call coincidences are events that coincide, like meeting someone who has the same name as you. However, everyone has a name, so the probability of meeting someone with the same name as yours, based on the number of people you'll meet over the course of your life, is actually quite high."

She shot him a challenging look as she folded her arms over her chest. "How many Faradays have you met?"

"Well, none, but I also don't get out much," he answered with a chirp. "My point is that although coincidences can be explained mathematically, when events like an invitation to study Mexican cuisine pops up on the heels of our conversation about just that topic, it's probably not a coincidence. It's most likely planned and a trap."

"Probably," Paris agreed. "There's only one way to find out, though." She nodded at the card in his paws, encouraging him to read it.

He brought his attention to the piece of embossed stationery and read aloud.

"Faraday, you are cordially invited to learn the art of Mexican cuisine from the world-renowned chef at Hotel Laguna Maldita in beautiful Tortugas Locas. Due to your and Paris Beaufont's devotion to your farm-to-table restaurant, Little Pleasures, the Ward family would like to gift you with this opportunity to advance your culinary knowledge. Please meet with your instructor in the kitchen and be prepared to learn from the very best. Your accommodations and meals are included during your stay. We hope you enjoy your time with us."

Faraday glanced up, taking in the satisfied expression on Paris' face. She appeared eager about the invitation, whereas he felt the opposite. Tension built in his chest. "Who do you think sent this?"

"Not the Ward family at Hotel Laguna Maldita," she replied.

"Someone who would know we require such an education," Faraday mused, mostly to himself. "Someone with extreme foresight, and also the ability to coordinate events and the desire to mastermind them."

"Maybe Father Time or Mother Nature?" Paris offered.

"Maybe," he muttered, not convinced Papa Creola or Mama Jamba was behind this. It felt like the work of someone else, someone more mysterious.

"Well, pack your suitcase, and don't forget to send me a postcard."

Faraday lowered the card. "Again, this is a trick, and we don't know who is orchestrating it. I could be walking into a deadly situation."

Paris winked at him. "Most likely. That's the reason I want the postcard: to ensure you're still alive."

"There are other, more effective ways of communication, you know."

"Yeah, but I don't think the string and cans will stretch between Mexico and Canada," Paris joked.

"Ha-ha. So, you're really encouraging me to show up at this hotel where I've been lured for a mysterious and possibly nefarious reason?"

"And learn how to make fajitas," Paris added.

Faraday considered the situation while staring out the bank of windows. He wasn't fearful as much as curious. Something felt right about it, but he didn't know why.

"Yes, it's suspicious, but you're the perfect person…I mean, squirrel, to investigate this situation," Paris continued. "Just remain alert. Look for clues and figure out why you're there. It isn't so you can learn about different peppers. My instinct tells me that whoever is behind this has a good motive, so instead of thinking of it as a trick, it might just be part of a clever plan."

Faraday flicked his tail, glad Paris had the same impression as him. "Yes, it's starting to feel like the work of one of our friends."

Paris flashed a smile, nodding. "I think so, too."

"Well, then I better go pack my sunscreen. Looks like I'm heading to Mexico. Can you open a portal for me to this Hotel Laguna Maldita?"

"Yes, but you're investigating and learning, not working on your tan," Paris answered. "And try not to rub it in my face that you get to go south to sunny weather while I'm trekking up to the North Pole to freeze my tail off."

Faraday twitched his nose, shaking his head at her. "Ha-ha. Very funny. We both know you don't have a tail, and I burn fast in the sun."

"You're a strange squirrel," Paris remarked dryly, taking a step back and opening a portal with minimal effort. It shimmered a bright blue, casting light around the bar area. There was a warning look in her eyes when she glanced back at Faraday. "Be careful, regardless."

"I will," he chirped, scurrying off the bar and in the direction of the portal that led to Hotel Laguna Maldita in Tortugas Locas, Mexico. "I might be a strange squirrel, but I'm also resourceful and observant, given my scientific nature."

"That you are," Paris said proudly. "In a nutshell, I'd say you're very smart."

Faraday shook his head, hiding his laugh as he hurried through the portal to the mysterious location. It would undoubtedly hold many puzzles to solve and dangers to avoid.

CHAPTER FOUR

Kaiser was very close to achieving the seemingly impossible. For how many centuries had he been trying and failing to take down his greatest adversary, only to be defeated by him?

Plato, the magical lynx, might have been granted a long life unlike any other, making him impossible to kill. However, Kaiser knew nothing was impossible, and he finally had what he needed to bring down Plato once and for all.

Kaiser didn't know how the mysterious lynx had become so powerful and acquired seemingly endless lives, but he suspected it was through deceit and treachery. The cat was a master of deception, which was how he'd taken Kaiser down all those years ago.

But the mogul was back and stronger than ever. Soon he'd destroy the city that had ridiculed him, the people who hadn't believed in him, and the creature who had taken it all from him.

Kaiser descended into the basement of his coastal mansion in Tortugas Locas. He detested the damp smell of the dark space. He had never liked living by the ocean, having grown up nearby, but soon the mildewing city of Tortugas Locas would be destroyed by a level-five hurricane. If that wasn't enough, the mobsters Kaiser had employed to take over the town would ensure the economy and tourist industry took a punch to the stomach.

But he wasn't deluding himself into thinking that would be enough. Those were only the carrots that would draw Plato out of hiding. The lynx wouldn't be able to resist intervening in the situation when his precious Tortugas Locas was in danger. The reason Plato was so fond of the city eluded Kaiser, but it was evident that he had a strong devotion to the place. The cat had said as much before he'd cast his power on Kaiser all those years ago and reduced him to nothing.

Catching his reflection in the bank of stainless-steel cabinets that lined one wall of the basement, Kaiser marveled. He didn't look anything like the man Plato had tried to destroy. He was a master of disguise, and his once-bald head was covered with thick black hair. The large mustache and beard concealed the many scars on his face. His years of strenuous exercise while imprisoned had shaped Kaiser into a new man. But his eyes? Well, they were the same, and they carried that glint of sinister desire he had been born with.

Pulling his gaze from his image, Kaiser centered his attention on the box that sat in the middle of the open space. It was three feet by three feet, a perfect cube. Like the metal cabinets along the wall, the container was covered in stainless steel. However, whereas the cabinets were full of supplies, the box was empty.

Pulling a remote from his pocket, Kaiser pressed a button on the top. The device in front of him, which was called the trapper cube, opened with a screech. A sense of emptiness seemed to take over the basement, but Kaiser shook that off, knowing it was the magitech from the device.

Hitting another button on the remote caused a bright light to flicker to life inside the trapper cube, and it grew in intensity with each passing second. That was the element that would draw in his prey. All Plato had to do was to be near the trapper cube, and that homing signal would attract him and draw the cat into the space. The signal was unique to Plato, so it would only trap him and no one else.

Tapping the bottom button on the remote created a piercing sound that filled the basement, making Kaiser's ears ache. However, he didn't cover them, too overcome by his excitement to care. The last facet of the trapper cube was the most crucial.

Catching Plato was key, but he had failed to do that in the past. However, the lynx wouldn't be able to resist being drawn into the box. Once in there, its regeneration blocker would be activated. That was how Plato had been able to avoid death all these centuries, Kaiser had learned. Every time he was injured or killed, the lynx regenerated to heal or come back to life. However, Kaiser had secured the technology to stop his magic, if only briefly. That was all Kaiser needed, though.

Once the regeneration blocker in the trapper cube was activated, all Kaiser had to do was deliver one deadly blow to the lynx. Then Plato would finally be gone...for good.

Kaiser pushed his suit jacket back with his free hand to reveal the pistol on his hip. It was his father's gun, the very one he'd killed him with, and it was the one Kaiser would use to shoot Plato, too. There would be no coming back for the magical lynx.

Kaiser laughed coldly, his voice echoing in the damp basement. Revenge was imminent, and it was overdue for the mastermind Plato.

CHAPTER FIVE

The humidity was the first thing Faraday noticed when he stepped through the portal into the lush yard that surrounded Hotel Laguna Maldita. The shimmering lagoon, which was rich with sea life and fascinating experiments, was the second thing. The five-story yellow stucco hotel with an infinity pool was the third thing.

A flicker of something blue on the rooftop caught Faraday's attention briefly but disappeared. He would have thought he had imagined it, given the blue sky overhead. However, flapping from the rooftop told him he probably *had* seen something.

Faraday was about to climb the stairs to the roof when bellowing voices from the open dining area stole his attention. Three men sitting around a table drinking were the source. Before Faraday even took in their appearances, he had deduced they were seedy characters based on their rude exchanges.

"You dumb idiot, Fishy Paul!" one of the men yelled, holding up his hand like he was going to slap the guy on his right. "We can't get through the back if there's a security guard. That's why Kevin Gruesome is crawling in through the second-floor window."

"But Donte, I'm afraid of heights," the third man said from the other side of the table.

Donte spun, his hand still raised. "Then get over it. We ain't got time for your bogus fears."

Kevin shrugged, looking defeated. "I don't understand why I have to be the one to climb to the second story of the warehouse."

"Because you're the shortest of us," Fishy Paul explained with a laugh. "Maybe if you grew some."

Donte chuckled. "Yeah…Kevin Gruesome!"

Though he slumped, Kevin appeared to be restraining himself. His eyes flickered over and caught sight of Faraday. "Hey, what you looking at, squirrel? Why don't you scat!"

The other men spun to stare at Faraday, who was standing a few yards away.

"What? Are you afraid of a puny squirrel now too?" Fishy Paul teased.

"Yeah, that mangy rodent might bite you, Kevin Gruesome," Donte added.

Realizing he shouldn't risk himself around these diabolical characters who were moments from pulling out guns and using Faraday for target practice, he scurried to the side of the hotel. He was on the hunt for the kitchen, where his training would start.

CHAPTER SIX

I t didn't take long for Faraday to sneak around to the front of the hotel and locate the kitchen. He just followed his nose. The smells of savory spices and roasting vegetables and fresh tortillas drew Faraday straight into the large room.

The stove was full of pots, their contents simmering, sautéing, or frying. As Faraday's nose had told him, tortillas were cooking on the griddle. A round woman with a worried expression mopped her brow as she buzzed between work surfaces, seemingly trying to remember what to do next.

Quietly, Faraday climbed onto the countertop at the woman's back and took a spot next to a large spice rack. He was fascinated by the small jars, which were filled with brightly colored spices that gave off rich aromas.

Faraday was surprised to see the invitation he'd been sent sitting next to the spice rack. He hadn't thought to bring it with him and realized that was an oversight. He'd probably need it to prove that he had been asked to come here.

Someone was working in the background to coordinate everything, but who that was? Well, that would involve more investigation.

Faraday returned his attention to the woman, who was muttering to herself absentmindedly as she stirred the pots, tasting their contents here and there.

After lifting a spoon out of a simmering pot of beans, she blew on it and took a small taste. "It needs more paprika."

Distractedly, she reached in Faraday's direction without looking. Springing into action, the squirrel grabbed the jar of bright red spice labeled Paprika and held it in the air over his head. The woman's fingers bumped into it before grasping the jar and taking it from him.

Glancing at the paprika, the chef of Hotel Laguna Maldita appeared surprised to have blindly picked up the right spice. She shrugged it off, however, not seeing Faraday next to the rack, and unscrewed the lid before sprinkling a bit into the pot. She stirred the beans once more before tasting them again.

"More cumin," she said, a question in her voice like she hoped someone would answer. Again, she reached over to the spice rack, glancing over her shoulder at a commotion coming from the dining area. The three men were getting rowdier, probably fighting over the next phase of their plan, which had sounded like a robbery to Faraday.

The woman sighed, the tension on her face evident and definitely connected to the presence of the rough guys in the dining room.

Quickly searching the spice rack, Faraday grabbed the jar of cumin and held it up like the paprika. The chef again took the jar, not seeing the small squirrel beneath it.

She sprinkled some cumin into the pot, again mopping her brow. Faraday thought her sweating was a result of her stress as well as the temperature in the kitchen. The chef at Hotel Laguna Maldita seemed like a nice woman with a sweet disposition, but something—or a few things—seemed to have her on edge. After another good stir, the woman tasted the beans again. "Oh, it needs a smidge of oregano."

She stirred the pot as she reached for the rack.

Faraday jerked around to search for the oregano. He located it but realized the container was empty. Swinging back to the chef, he looked up, his big eyes full of remorse.

"You're all out of oregano," he told her.

Shocked, the chef spun to face him, then jumped back several feet, brandishing her wooden spoon like a weapon. She blinked, taking in the talking squirrel on her countertop. Faraday, hoping to put her fears to rest, smiled and held up the empty jar.

He shook it. "See? You're out of oregano."

The plump woman closed her eyes. "Dear God, I'm hallucinating. Please help me."

"What did you see?" Faraday looked around the kitchen for something dangerous.

The chef opened her eyes and blinked at the squirrel. "You. You're a figment of my imagination. You can talk."

He nodded. "Yeah, a science experiment that went wrong…or one might say, very right. Anyway, I can talk. You can cook. My name is Faraday. And you are…"

"Francesca," she supplied.

"We're all caught up, then." Faraday smiled at her good-naturedly. "We can get to my first lesson."

"First lesson?" She tilted her head in confusion.

"Yeah, for my training in Mexican cooking." He picked up the embossed card sitting on the countertop next to him and held it out to her.

With a shaking hand, she grabbed it from the squirrel as if he might turn rabid and bite her.

Her eyes ran over the raised print, and she read out loud.

"Faraday, you are cordially invited to learn the art of Mexican cuisine from the world-renowned chef at Hotel Laguna Maldita in beautiful Tortugas Locas. Due to your and Paris Beaufont's devotion to your farm-to-table restaurant, Little Pleasures, the Ward family would like to

gift you with this opportunity to advance your culinary knowledge. Please meet with your instructor in the kitchen and be prepared to learn from the very best. Your accommodations and meals are included during your stay. We hope you enjoy your time with us."

She lowered the card with confusion on her face. "I didn't send this."

"You're the chef here?" Faraday asked.

She nodded. "Francesca Ward."

"You're an expert in Mexican cuisine?"

"I guess. I mean, I'm not sure about being an expert. You have a farm-to-table restaurant? You're a talking squirrel." That was obviously still hard for Francesca to digest.

"Yes, and my sidekick is a fairy godmother." He added, "Although I believe Paris thinks of me as *her* sidekick. Don't tell her it's the other way around."

Francesca mopped her brow with a cloth. "Oh, my. Fairy godmothers, talking squirrels, mobsters, and ghosts. I can't take anymore."

"Did you say mobsters and ghosts?" Faraday had thought the guys in the open dining room were mobster types. They weren't up to any good, and he'd thought they must be part of the problem he'd been recruited for. This ghost might be the other problem.

She nodded and pointed at the dining room, where the commotion was getting louder. "Yeah, they took over the hotel today. Then the ghost... Well, my husband says it's the boiler acting up, but I think it's an upset ghost."

"I could take a look at the boiler if you'd like," Faraday offered, thinking that sounded like an easier problem than ghosts and mobsters.

"You're a squirrel," she countered, a questioning look on her face.

"A science experiment that went right, remember? I know

things."

"And you cook," Francesca added speculatively.

"Well, no one else could take the opportunity when you sent it, so I was elected."

"I didn't send it."

"Right," Faraday chirped. "Someone lured me here. It sounds like you need help. Maybe I'll stick around for a bit and keep an eye on things. Paris is on a solo mission and doesn't need my help, so I might as well offer you my expertise. Like that boiler, for instance."

Francesca waved him off. "A scientist checked into the hotel today and offered to take a look at it today."

"Today. A scientist…" Faraday flicked his tail, thinking. "Yeah, I'll need to look into this."

"No one can see you running around this place," Francesca told him forcefully. "I mean, if anyone reported that we have rodents…well, that's a huge problem. And if someone sees a talking squirrel? Well, we already have a ghost."

"Leave it to me, Francesca. No one will see me. I'm the master of stealth. If you have a problem with your boiler or a ghost, I'll help you."

"You will?" She softened. "But why? Why help us?"

He smiled. "Because you seem like a good person who is trying to follow your passion, and someone led me here to help you. I don't know why or how, but my instincts tell me that I should."

"That's a very odd thing for a squirrel to say," she admitted after a long pause.

"I assure you that I almost never say what you'd expect a squirrel to say."

"Which is nothing," she added with a laugh.

Faraday laughed too, realizing there were things he could help with at Hotel Laguna Maldita. The question was still, who had recruited him?

There was something wrong with the boiler, Faraday observed as he snuck into the space. The large contraption was vibrating violently as if it were gearing up to launch into the sky like a rocket. Steam issued from the bottom of the device, obscuring a portion of the room.

That was why Faraday didn't see the other person in the room until they started talking. He darted into the shadows in a corner, out of view, and in a perfect place for spying.

When the steam cleared, Faraday got a look at the figure. It was the scientist Francesca described when he'd asked her about the person. Her name was Doctor Beth Hailey, and although she incessantly talked to herself, she'd been nice enough to offer to fix the boiler when she heard about the issue upon checking in.

Dr. Hailey seemed nutty as she stooped and unscrewed something from the side of the boiler, shaking her long red hair. "He better pay up when I make this machine..." the woman muttered, grunting as she worked with a wrench to loosen a bolt.

Machine? Faraday thought, wondering what the madwoman was talking about. Something thudded against an adjacent wall, making both the squirrel and woman tense. Faraday glanced at the wall, wondering what could have made that noise. It wasn't the boiler, based on its proximity.

Dr. Hailey shook her head and returned to her work. "This is a rundown dump. The sooner I'm done with this hurricane machine, the sooner I'm out of here."

Hurricane machine! Faraday thought, piecing the scheme together.

"Then I'm taking my cash payment and retreating to a *real* paradise." Dr. Hailey stared dreamily into the distance. "Someplace like Prague or Budapest, or maybe even Glasgow."

Faraday cringed, wondering how those places could be considered paradises in comparison to the warm beaches and sparkling water in Mexico.

Dr. Hailey straightened, picking up the tool kit beside her. She glanced at the boiler, which was whistling even more violently than moments prior. "It appears I have everything I need to start the hurricane machine." She pointed at an open area like she was talking to someone in the room. "I'll construct it right there. But first, I'll go retrieve my blueprints. Then dinner. Then we begin."

We? Faraday thought, realizing Dr. Hailey was a few bolts short of being all there.

After the scientist marched out of the boiler room, Faraday saw what she'd been doing. The madwoman hadn't been trying to fix the boiler. It was obvious under inspection that she'd been stripping vital equipment from it, which was causing its malfunction to get worse. If the boiler hadn't had problems before, it did now.

A howl that hadn't come from the simmering boiler echoed through the room and shook the walls. Faraday tensed. If the boiler wasn't the cause of the noise and had only recently malfunctioned, what was causing the commotion?

CHAPTER EIGHT

"I told you, we have a ghost," Francesca explained while chopping an onion. She made quick work of dicing the pungent vegetable into tiny pieces.

"That's one explanation," Faraday stated, using the mortar and pestle to grind some spices and herbs. It was a lot of work for the little squirrel, but he liked the chore and the smell the freshly ground mix gave off. "But scientifically speaking, there's no evidence to support the presence of a ghost, so I was thinking that there might be another cause for the disruptions."

Francesca sighed. "Sometimes science can't explain things."

Faraday hid his annoyance. "In my world, that's not true."

"Love, then," Francesca challenged, moving on to chopping a line of colorful peppers. "Scientifically explain to me how love happens. How does a person fall so madly in love with another person that they will do anything for them?"

"Well, evolutionarily speaking, we're governed by hormones," Faraday began in a clinical tone. "You see, pheromones create a breeding ground if you will. Then we have oxytocin, which attracts mothers to children, and—"

"The moment I saw Jack across a crowded restaurant, I knew

I would spend my life with him," Francesca interrupted. "Explain that. Explain how I picked up on his pheromones over all the other people's in the room."

"Well, I'm sure there's a reasonable explanation," Faraday squeaked.

"And then we started talking, and I felt like I'd always known him," Francesca continued, a faraway expression in her eyes as she spoke about her husband. "And although I'd never left my hometown, I moved to the United States for him. Then, even though he had only ever known his life there, he moved here for me. How does science explain sacrifices and devotion like that?"

"Well…" Faraday glanced down at his spice mix, suddenly and strangely at a loss for a reasonable explanation.

Francesca was smiling warmly at him when he looked up. "You see, sometimes science can't explain things, but that doesn't make them any less true. Love exists, even if science can't define it. And so does that ghost."

"I honestly can't agree without evidence," Faraday stated. Not a second later, a jar of marjoram flew through the air, nearly hitting Francesca in the head and shattering against the far wall. Faraday and the chef jumped and the squirrel whipped around, looking for what had thrown the glass. There was nothing there.

Gulping, Faraday brought his gaze up to meet Francesca's.

"How is that for evidence?" she challenged.

"That will do." His tone was filled with nervousness.

Faraday nearly jumped again when Laura, Francesca's ten-year-old daughter, skipped into the kitchen, her pigtails flopping.

"Can I have something to eat, Mama?"

"You just ate, child." Francesca collected herself with steadying breaths, her gaze on the broken glass beside the far wall.

"I'm still hungry," Laura protested.

"Between you and those mobsters, we'll be out of food in no

time," Francesca complained, but she wiped her hands on her apron, strode over to the refrigerator, and opened it.

"They are really going on about something right now," Laura said in a hushed voice, looking at Faraday with curiosity. She'd met him briefly and hadn't seemed as surprised about a talking squirrel as he would have expected. "That new waiter you hired is having trouble keeping them from disturbing the other guests."

Francesca sighed as she looked into the refrigerator. "What happened to that rack of lamb? I could have sworn it was in here."

"Oh, I ate that," Laura admitted, her face turning pink.

Spinning, her mother gave her a look of shock. "You what?"

"I ate it," Laura repeated. "I was really hungry late last night."

"So, you ate a whole rack of lamb?" Faraday had to ask.

The girl nodded.

Francesca pulled a cooked roast out of the refrigerator, shaking her head. "Well, you're definitely going through a growth spurt. Take this to the dining room for a snack. With everything going on, I can't have you going hungry. I need you at your best, child."

Laura took the large platter, sinking under its weight. "Thanks, Mama. I'll stay out of your way. I promise."

"That would be good." Francesca wiped her brow as her daughter left the kitchen.

"You really think she ate a whole rack of lamb?" Faraday questioned.

"Who knows?" Francesca shrugged. "She might have only had some and put the rest in the trash. Children's eyes are always bigger than their stomachs. But Laura and her growth spurt are the least of my problems. If she ate the rack of lamb, it's one less thing for those mobsters to steal from us. I've also got the boiler issues and the ghost and the smoke."

"Smoke?" Faraday asked.

"Yeah, I smelled smoke all today. I could have sworn the hotel was on fire earlier, which almost gave me a heart attack. There is just too much to deal with. I really hope you're able to help with the boiler and maybe even the ghost."

Faraday nodded. He was off in thought, piecing the puzzle together. "Yes. I think I'll be able to help, but first, I have to do a bit of reconnaissance work."

CHAPTER NINE

The sun was high in the Mexican sky when Faraday climbed up over the edge of the roof of Hotel Laguna Maldita. He held up a small monocle that he'd fashioned from found materials to create a glamour-off lens, the term he'd coined for the device he'd one day patent. It saw through most glamours, but one had to know to use it and where since looking through the lens often wasn't advised. That could be detrimental to one's eyes.

The glamour-off lens transformed the pile of patio furniture before Faraday's eyes. Instead of being a mound of lawn chairs and umbrellas, it was revealed to be a large sleeping blue dragon.

Lunis, the dragon who belonged to Sophia Beaufont, yawned before shuffling to attention, but his actions came too little too late. Faraday regarded him with an expression that said, "You've been caught."

"As I suspected. You can take down your glamour, Lunis. I see you."

Realizing the squirrel did see him, Lunis dropped the glamour and materialized with a wide grin. That allowed Faraday to lower the glamour-off lens.

"Well, hey there, Faraday. Did you win an all-inclusive vacation to this place too?"

The squirrel shook his head, climbed over the ledge, and scurried to the dragon. The pair had worked together on other missions, and as Beaufonts, they knew each other well.

"No, I received an invitation to learn Mexican cooking. Surprisingly, I didn't apply for the opportunity. How about you?"

"Yeah, it was like the package dropped magically into my lap." Lunis sniffed the air. "Do you smell a rat?"

"More like a feline." Faraday snickered.

"How did you know I was up here?"

"Well, although Laura is growing, I didn't buy that the twelve-year-old ate an entire rack of lamb. That was what she tried to convince her mother of when it went missing."

Lunis licked his chops. "That rack of lamb was delicious."

"Then I put together that someone had lured me here. I believe it was Plato," Faraday continued.

The blue dragon nodded. "Oh, yes, this whole situation reeks of the magical lynx."

"I figured that if Plato lured me here to solve the goings-on, he might've also recruited you."

"Yes, my dear Watson. I think your observation is accurate."

Faraday grimaced and crossed his tiny arms. "Why do you get to be Sherlock Holmes in this scenario?"

"Isn't it obvious?"

"Not really," Faraday grumped.

"Because I smoke a pipe." Lunis held an imaginary pipe to his mouth and blew out smoke rings.

The squirrel laughed. "That's the other way I figured you out. Francesca said she kept smelling smoke when tidying up the lawn area, and I heard flapping."

"Hey, you couldn't expect me to eat the rack of lamb raw. I'm a dragon, not a savage."

Faraday nodded. "So, you smoked it. That makes sense."

"I have a related question for you." Lunis hid a grin.

"I'm certain you don't," the squirrel replied dryly.

"If we are what we eat, does that make you nuts?"

Faraday didn't laugh. Instead, he shook his head. "I saw that joke coming a mile away. You know I'm allergic to nuts."

"Right, because that's not weird for a squirrel."

"I talk," Faraday countered. "That's what makes me weird."

"Plus, that whole science thing you do." Lunis indicated the monocle hanging from Faraday's neck.

"Yes, and I've deduced that my science background is one of the reasons Plato enlisted my help," Faraday explained. "I discovered a strange magitech scientist stripping the boiler of essential parts. From what I've observed, she's trying to create a machine that will generate a hurricane."

Lunis looked at the brooding storm clouds overhead. "Looks like she might be succeeding. Did you recognize the machine she's working on? Is that how you know she intends to create a hurricane?"

Faraday shook his head. "No, the nutter talks to herself incessantly. She mumbled that some man hired her to build the machine. Doctor Beth Hailey doesn't plan to create the full hurricane, but her testing has created the potential for a storm. I suspect it will only get worse."

Lunis huffed. "Oh, great. Maybe I can get a room inside the hotel."

"I doubt it. That's the other problem brewing in the hotel. Have you heard about the mobsters who have taken over in there?"

"Yeah, Laura told me about them."

Faraday nodded. "Yeah, their wrath is getting worse, and the family is suffering. They intimidate all the guests and make a lot of unreasonable demands."

"The greedy little jerks need to be taught a lesson."

Faraday flicked his tail. "I agree. On top of that, I think a ghost is haunting the hotel. Jack thinks the malfunctioning boiler is the cause of the knocking noises in the walls. However, the boiler didn't have any problems until Dr. Hailey started stripping parts from it. As Francesca said, I've seen objects fly off shelves and the exterior walls shaking."

"Which wouldn't be the case if it was a boiler issue," Lunis mused, combing his claws over his chin like a detective thinking about a case.

"Yes, so I thought we could do some research on Hotel Laguna Maldita," Faraday continued. "The family doesn't know anything about the place. Neither one of us can quiz the locals to get information."

"Because talking squirrels and dragons freak mortals out," Lunis laughed.

"Exactly," Faraday chirped. "So, I can take a trip to the Great Library and see if Paul, the Great Librarian, can help me find history on this place. If someone recorded it, it is there."

Lunis gauged the dark clouds overhead again. "You better hurry on that one because something tells me we don't have long."

An old leather-bound book appeared beside the two magical creatures, followed by a *pop*. They swung around, looking alert, and their eyes darted to the book sitting on the rooftop.

Faraday arched an eyebrow at Lunis. "That book wasn't there a moment ago, was it?"

"I don't believe so, my dear Watson."

"Again, why do you get to be Sherlock?" Faraday complained. "You tell too many bad jokes to be the great detective."

"Just for that, I'm not entertaining you with any of my jokes, and you pronounced 'awesome' wrong."

Lunis made his way to the book in one step while it took Faraday several hops. The blue dragon leaned over the tome, flipping to a marked page. His eyes widened. "Watson. Come at once if convenient. If inconvenient, come all the same."

Faraday hurried around to the other side of the book, which the large blue dragon mostly blocked. It appeared to be a history of Tortugas Locas. "So, you've given up jokes to quote Sherlock Holmes now? How do you know those?"

Lunis looked up from the book and winked. "My name is Sherlock Holmes. It is my business to know what other people don't know."

Faraday laughed. "Wow, I set you up perfectly for that."

Lunis tapped the book with his claw. "Look at this. It's the history of Hotel Laguna Maldita."

Faraday's gaze scanned the words as he muttered, "Built in… blah…blah…blah…" He skipped down several passages. "Owner-ship changed hands several times…blah…blah…blah…"

"Wow, take a speed-reading class." Lunis laughed and pointed at the bottom of the page. "Down here is the story of our ghost, I believe." He cleared his throat and began to read from the book.

"*A baron by the name of Fabien Coulter stole his family's fortune, enraging his six older brothers. Fabien escaped to Tortugas Locas to 'live like a king' and avoid being hunted down by his siblings. He moved into Hotel Laguna Maldita and lived a lavish lifestyle with dozens of servants, famous guests, and rich foods.*

"*However, it didn't last long. The Coulter brothers tracked him down, retrieved the stolen riches, locked him in the hotel, surrounded it, and declared that if he tried to leave, one of the brothers would kill him on the spot. Left with nothing but the hotel and sparse rations, Fabien Coulter lasted only ten days before taking his life.*"

Faraday's chin jerked up, his eyes wide. "It's the baron who haunts the hotel. That makes perfect sense."

"It appears this saved you the time and trouble of going to the Great Library for research."

"Yes, thanks, Plato," Faraday called over his shoulder.

Lunis snickered. "In truth, I think the real Sherlock Holmes is that magical lynx."

"I suspect you're correct," Faraday mused. "So, we have a mad scientist creating a hurricane, a boiler that's about to blow, three mobsters creating trouble, and an angry ghost. I see why Plato recruited us, but how do you suppose he expects us to fix all those problems?"

"There is nothing more deceptive than an obvious fact." Lunis pretended to smoke a pipe again.

"Would you stop quoting Sherlock Holmes and say what you mean?" Faraday insisted.

"We could take down each of our three villains," Lunis began. "I'm confident that we could. Or we could use them to take each other down."

Faraday gasped. "Yes, of course. That would be a Plato strategy. Why fight your enemies when you can make them fight each other?"

"Elementary, my dear Watson." Lunis winked at the squirrel.

Faraday tapped his chin with his paw while considering. "Okay, I think I have a plan that could isolate our villains together and get rid of them before they create much more trouble."

Lunis leaned close. "Okay, I'm ready to hear your plan and take full credit for its brilliance."

CHAPTER TEN

The artificially created storm assaulted Tortugas Locas with high winds and sideways rain. The hotel staff had worked fast to board up the place as best as they could. There was usually more warning about tropical storms, but in this case, there had been almost none.

The torrential winds hadn't been enough to quiet the mobsters, who now seemed more on edge like the storm was fueling them. The brewing hurricane seemed to be heightening everyone's emotions. The ghost of Baron Fabien Coulter was such a force that even Faraday couldn't explain away his presence. The angry ghost vibrated the walls and howled through the halls, but his voice was often drowned out by the storm like the two were competing for attention.

Faraday knew this meant things were coming to a head. It was time to pit their enemies against each other as he and Lunis had planned. His part wasn't easy and would take a lot of precision, but science was his specialty.

The one aspect of the plan Faraday didn't like was stealing. However, it was crucial for things to go right. When Jack Ward wasn't looking, the little squirrel had taken the keys to the motorboat out in the lagoon from his pocket. When the lobby was empty save for Emmanuel, the new waiter, and Laura doing her homework, Faraday dropped the keys on the counter in the lobby just before Donte and his goons stormed into the room.

Faraday jumped out of sight, having set the stage. He was sure that three mobsters looking for transportation to what seemed like the perfect heist would take the bait. The next part of taking out those criminals was up to Lunis.

Faraday's other tasks included stopping the mad scientist, her hurricane, and the ghost from destroying Hotel Laguna Maldita. He scurried to the boiler room as thunder rocked the floor, hoping he hadn't waited too long to stop the storm or contain the ghost. This part of the plan relied on timing.

Doctor Beth Hailey confined her long red hair in her hands and regarded the hurricane machine vengefully. The force and magic issuing from the device had blown out the bank of windows along one wall. That was when the magical hurricane had entered the atmosphere, cycling as it built up and became a real storm. Faraday had watched it intensify, knowing it wasn't yet time to intervene. He'd get his window, then he'd have to act fast, or everything would be lost. *Everything.*

Wind and sprays of water shot into the open space. The howling from the storm made it almost impossible to hear the raging scientist.

"You weren't supposed to do this!" Dr. Hailey pulled her hair and ran around the large machine she'd created beside the nonfunctional boiler. The scientist had stripped the boiler, so no one would be taking a warm shower. However, most would think that was because of the hurricane approaching the shores.

"It was supposed to be a test!" the redhead yelled, throwing her hands at the machine. It hissed in reply.

The baron, who was still beating on the walls, seemed more likely to have a conversation. Dr. Hailey swung around and regarded the bricks of the exterior wall as she muttered, "There are no boiler issues, so what's making that noise?"

On cue, as if he were waiting to be invited, a ghostly face poked through the bricks. His eyes were sunken. His blond hair came to his chin, and he wore a regal outfit befitting a nineteenth-century French nobleman. However, his transparent white appearance made it obvious that he hadn't been in this world for a very long time.

"You dare to terrorize my home?" Baron Fabien Coulter boomed, mouth wide and voice echoing,

Dr. Hailey screamed. Her hands flew to her hair, and her eyes widened in horror. "You're a-a-a ghost!"

"And you're dead!" Baron Fabien Coulter threatened, his hands extended as though he was going to strangle the scientist.

CHAPTER TWELVE

Faraday went into action. The ghost was taking care of the scientist for him, getting both out of his hair so he could work on the hurricane machine. The wind that raced around the device knocked the little rodent off his feet several times, but he managed to jump to a safe place and get back to work.

However, after completing half the rewiring for the "new" device that wouldn't be a boiler or a hurricane machine, Faraday realized the ghost was back. Thankfully, he appeared to have taken most of his anger out on the mad scientist, who had screamed and run toward the lagoon. Faraday had deduced that the ghost wouldn't be able to leave the hotel and would be back soon, but he had hoped to make more progress on the new device before Fabien returned.

Unfortunately, the baron's ghost hadn't cooled down enough for Faraday's liking after chasing off Dr. Hailey. He was more enraged than before, screaming as he beat his chest. The volume of his voice shook the hotel's foundation, throwing Faraday off-balance.

The squirrel dove to avoid debris that flew in from the storm, then found a safe place on the machine's far side, where he continued his tinkering.

"My home has been invaded!" Baron Fabien Coulter exclaimed. "I won't put up with it any longer! If I can't live here in peace, no one will. I'll demolish the place."

Plaster fell from the walls. A crack ran up the bricks to the ceiling. It sounded like the roof was going to cave in.

Faraday glanced at the hurricane machine nervously, then caught the gaze of Baron Coulter. "If you could give me one more minute? I have a surprise for you."

CHAPTER THIRTEEN

Faraday had halted the baron. The ghost, whether not accustomed to being spoken to by a squirrel or not spoken to at all, paused. It wouldn't last long.

Thankfully, the hurricane machine had been deactivated, and the storm outside the hotel was dying down naturally. However, converting the machine from one that created storms to one that sucked up paranormal creatures was new territory. Usually, a project of this magnitude would take the squirrel months, but he had less than that. The only thing that allowed him to be optimistic was, he had deduced that the hurricane machine had the same parts one needed for ghost-hunting.

This wasn't a project that Faraday, the squirrel scientist, had ever envisioned working on. He specialized in facts and data, not translucent entities that couldn't be detected and had little scientific evidence to support their existence. However, he couldn't doubt what his eyes saw or his ears heard or his body felt. The baron was real, and Faraday had to get rid of him.

The foundation quaked, nearly tossing Faraday upside-down, but he held on to the device before him, hopefully soon to be his salvation from this situation. The storm was dissipating, which meant the shaking walls and howling were due to the angry ghost.

"One more wire and we should have it," Faraday muttered to himself, feeling like the crazy Dr. Hailey, who babbled nonstop alone.

Usually, Faraday would want to test a new piece of equipment, especially something of this magnitude that could have dangerous repercussions if it backfired. But as the ghost barreled around the large boiler, Faraday knew that buying more time was out of the question.

He stamped his tiny foot down on the lever he'd created and squeezed his eyes shut as he held his breath and said a prayer, a strange activity for him. What happened next wasn't a miracle. It was the result of science and the coordination of some incredibly talented creatures.

CHAPTER FOURTEEN

The device that had unleashed a storm that created a hurricane reversed. It created a force that sucked up anything that had ethereal energy. Programming that into the machine had been one of Faraday's most complex tasks.

The squirrel cracked one eye open as more howls swirled through the air. He was shocked to find the ghost of Baron Fabien Coulter whirling around the boiler room like he was caught in a cyclone. Then the transparent figure was siphoned into the machine on the floor, his arms reaching for the ceiling in one last attempt to regain his freedom.

But it was too late.

The ghost who had lived a life of scandal, then terrorized Hotel Laguna Maldita for so long was forced into a new home, one created to build a storm that was now gone.

The temperature had risen by at least twenty degrees in the last few minutes, and it had nothing to do with the storm beating against Hotel Laguna Maldita. It had everything to do with what Faraday, the scientific squirrel, had done to the hurricane machine.

The magitech that had created the storm currently waging

war on the lagoon looked ready to burst. However, Faraday had things under control even if he was scurrying around the machine, pressing buttons and doing scientific things.

The most important thing was that aside from the wind battering the hotel, the building was quiet. The shaking due to paranormal activity was gone. The howling due to the long-running haunting had stopped.

The ghost of Baron Fabien Coulter was no more, thanks to what Faraday, the squirrel scientist, had done.

CHAPTER FIFTEEN

"So, that's what happened." Faraday finished telling his part of his story to Plato and Lunis.

The pair blinked at him across the bar table, neither appearing surprised. They were, however, impressed.

"Well, then, we've heard everyone's side of the story." Lunis drained his glass of whisky.

Emmanuel, the waiter, returned with another bottle of whisky, setting it down on the table wordlessly before trotting back to the bar.

"I don't think we've heard *everyone's* story," Plato said in a loud voice, and the people in the hotel lobby went quiet like a fight was about to break out. All attention turned to the three magical creatures in the corner.

"No?" Lunis asked, a teasing quality in his voice. "Well, should we open this new bottle of whisky and rehash all the tales, then?"

"You mean, the whisky we didn't order?" Faraday questioned, his calculating eyes studying the bottle in front of him.

"I guess it's just because we saved the day," Lunis continued jovially.

"It's been opened," Faraday stated, indicating the broken seal on the bottle.

"Right," Plato chirped. "But we weren't meant to drink it. I think it's an invitation."

"To?" Lunis questioned, casually glancing around.

Plato rose to his feet. "Fellows, I believe our chess game has only just begun. It appears that the person who has been orchestrating things all along has decided to show his face and finally step foot onto the board."

The lynx turned around, his gaze directed to the shore, where a plane was idling on the water. Standing beside it was a familiar face, the one person no one would have expected to be behind all the events that had led them to this moment.

"Of course, the diabolical evil villain is Emmanuel, the boring waiter," Lunis stated, rising to his feet.

"His name is Kaiser," Plato told his friends, watching as the man with the mustache and beard jumped into the plane and took off toward the coast on the other side of the lagoon. "And he shouldn't be underestimated. I only saw some of this coming, and the parts I haven't seen? Well, they make me very nervous."

CHAPTER SIXTEEN

The three watched as the plane retreated into the distance, growing smaller.

Lunis sighed and looked at Faraday and Plato. "Looks like we're going to need a ride. Can one of you call an Uber?"

Faraday groaned. "Seriously, dragon? Will you please give us a lift?"

The blue dragon grumbled, "Okay, fine. But in the next adventure, I get to be the smart one like you or the lead like Plato. It's hard, always having to be the mode of transportation."

"Who tells jokes," Faraday added as Lunis started toward the lawn to give himself a place to spread his wings. The patrons in the bar watched in awe as the cat and the squirrel boarded the dragon to take flight after the plane.

"And looks super handsome doing it," Lunis added. "Go ahead and hold on tightly. This is going to be a hell of a ride, brothers."

"Because the storm winds are still bad?" Faraday asked.

Lunis shook his head as he took off at a run, his wings flapping. He rose into the night air over the dark lagoon. "No, because I'm madder than hell. That guy set a trap, and we're about to teach him a lesson. Okay, although this will be a short trip, Plato, I want the lowdown on this Kaiser. I like to know why I'm pummeling people before I do."

"Well, he is one of those who was born bad," Plato stated. "In one of my past lives, I found refuge here in Tortugas Locas, and the people kept me safe."

"Was this during the Salem witch trials when talking cats were persecuted?" Lunis asked as the winds raced over them. Faraday held on tightly, finding refuge behind one of Lunis' horns.

"Something like that," Plato answered. "Since then, I've kept an eye on this place and helped it stay safe. At one point, I learned that Kaiser, one of its citizens, was out to harm the city, so I stopped him."

"Like, a slap on the wrist?" Lunis asked.

"Like public humiliation, imprisonment, and the loss of all assets and magical powers," Plato answered.

Lunis blew out a breath. "Man, don't mess with that feline. He will take it *all*."

"I knew Kaiser would be back, and I suspected he was behind all this," Plato continued.

"It would have been cool if you had given us a heads-up," Lunis stated.

"I don't do heads-ups," Plato said.

"Fine, fine." Lunis swerved, following the path of the plane. It had landed at a large estate next to the coast.

"So, Kaiser is leading us to his headquarters," Faraday stated. "Do you know what he has in store for us? It could be a trap."

"It most assuredly is," Plato stated, his voice heavy. "But that's a risk we're going to have to take. And although I think Kaiser is a worthy adversary, there's something in this scenario he hasn't accounted for."

"And that is?" Faraday questioned.

Plato looked at him, a glint in his eyes. "You two. Kaiser doesn't have friends and will never guess that mine will be my saving grace as I finally end this battle."

CHAPTER SEVENTEEN

"I don't think Emmanuel bought this place with his tips as a waiter," Lunis remarked as they flew over the huge mansion that stretched over a large tract of fenced land overlooking the Gulf of Mexico.

"Emmanuel wasn't real, and he was in disguise as a waiter," Faraday explained over the rush of wind as they circled the property. The house easily had a hundred rooms. The grounds consisted of tennis courts, multiple swimming pools, sprawling gardens, and a landing strip for the plane, which was now idling, its passenger having disembarked and run off.

"Yeah, Kaiser knows how to make money," Plato imparted, scanning the grounds for the man. "If he could have used his talents for good, the world would be a different place, but he's evil to his core."

"And he appears to be a master of stealth," Lunis grumbled, angling his wings to dive under the storm wind. "Where did that judge-y waiter go? How dare he question how much whisky I drank?"

"He's there!" Faraday exclaimed, having located the inconspicuous man standing in what looked like a lifeguard tower, which was two stories high. The area where he stood was perplexing.

"Is that a chessboard?" Faraday asked, looking at the checkered lawn in front of the tower composed of squares of green grass and marble tiles. On the oversized board were large statues of chess players—rooks, knights, pawns, and the rest of the pieces, lined up for a game.

"Yes, I should have expected this," Plato said through clenched teeth.

"Why would you expect this?" Lunis questioned, continuing to circle as they got a lay of the land.

"Because the way I took Kaiser down originally involved a very real game of chess," Plato answered.

"I'm guessing he lost," Faraday added.

The lynx nodded.

"I was playing chess with a friend the other day," Lunis began, a hint of laughter in his tone. "He said, 'Hey, let's make this interesting.' So, we stopped playing chess."

Faraday groaned. "That was bad. And chess is a riveting game, I'll have you know."

"Says the squirrel who thinks solving a sheet of math problems is a fun Saturday night," Lunis teased.

"That does sound like a delightful way to spend an evening," Faraday agreed.

"Well, after I torch the tower where Fake Waiter is stupidly hanging out, do you two want to play a game of chess?" Lunis questioned.

Plato shook his head. "If I know Kaiser, that tower is impenetrable. It will be shielded by magitech."

"I thought that you said he didn't have magic anymore?" Faraday questioned.

"He doesn't," Plato stated. "I shut it down to teach him a lesson, but if he's back and seeking revenge, he will be employing the best magitech money could buy."

"So, I can't blow him up," Lunis muttered. "He's hanging out in his tower like Rapunzel. Do you think he'll let down his beard for us?"

"I think he intends for me to play him in a rematch," Plato stated, his furious eyes on Kaiser in the tower. The mogul was regarding him with the same contempt.

"Well, again, this is a trap, and we're playing by his rules on his turf," Lunis argued. "I say that instead, I go and uproot all the palm trees on his pretty little property and line them up in front of his door, making it impossible for him to go inside."

"That only sounds mildly annoying," Faraday stated. "He'll figure out a way around them fairly quickly."

"I find the best way to break people down is through a series of mildly annoying gestures," Lunis teased.

"Kaiser tried to destroy Tortugas Locas with a hurricane and a bunch of greedy mobsters," Plato seethed. "You both know we have to uphold justice, which means bringing this man down once and for all. Who knows what other diabolical plans he has in the works? No, it's evident that I have to stop Kaiser from creating any more problems for this world. Land us, Lunis. It's time to end this."

CHAPTER EIGHTEEN

Landing gracefully and skillfully, Lunis shook his head like a dog after a bath. Plato slid off the wing opposite Faraday and stood at the corner of the chessboard. It stretched between the three and the tower where Kaiser stood, some fifty yards away.

Faraday jumped off Lunis, and the blue dragon folded his wings. He towered over his friends as they faced the villain in the distance, who had a proud look on his face.

"It's been a long time, Plato." Kaiser's voice was loud and clear and full of disdain.

"Maybe for you," Plato stated nonchalantly, like he was bored by the whole situation.

Even from afar, Faraday saw the man narrow his eyes. "Yes, that's right: you, the magical lynx who has lived for centuries. For you, time means nothing. That's why you wouldn't understand how it affected me when I was reduced to a mortal, stripped of my magic by you, and imprisoned for decades."

"It must have been mildly annoying," Lunis joked, steam issuing from his nostrils.

Kaiser cut his eyes to Lunis. "Your friends aren't going to be able to help you."

"I'm certain they will," Plato stated with confidence. "They already stopped the hurricane and the mobsters you tried to use to destroy Tortugas Locas."

Kaiser laughed, a cold, hollow sound. "Those were just side projects to lure you here. I knew you couldn't stand by while your precious Tortugas Locas was attacked. But while you've been trying to save that repugnant city, I was laying the framework for its demise."

"You think I don't know you've been planting bombs all over this city?" Plato challenged.

The look of pride slid off Kaiser's face. "Well, it appears you know some of what I've got in store. However, I'm certain you don't know everything I've been up to."

"How can you be so sure?" Plato asked.

Kaiser held up a small black remote, a wicked expression on his face. "Because if you did, you wouldn't be standing there right now."

CHAPTER NINETEEN

The click of one of the buttons on the remote seemed to echo for miles. Faraday tensed, expecting a bomb to go off beside them.

Instead, a large silver box in the middle of the chessboard screeched open. Faraday hadn't noticed the box among the stone chess pieces. It was three feet by three feet and took up an entire tile.

Perplexed by the strange feeling of hollowness that filled his chest, Faraday tried to figure out what the box was for. It was a complex piece of magitech.

Kaiser held up the remote and sneered. "It's time to trap the seemingly untrappable lynx. Time to know what it's like to be caged, Plato."

Faraday spun to look at his friend, ready to spring into action. However, three things happened in unison, creating chaos.

The first was that the pieces from the chessboard came to life and shuffled in their direction. Faraday realized they were magitech as well. Lunis jumped forward protectively, putting his wings out to guard his friends when a knight barreled in their direction, menace written on its robotic horse-face. Finally, Plato rose into the air above their heads, trying to resist the force that had control of him but unable to fight it.

Kaiser cackled as Plato flew toward the open, glowing silver box. Lunis glanced up, terror in his eyes as his friend was yanked away from them. However, he was fighting off a knight, a couple of rooks, and a pawn that had him cornered. Faraday darted between the strange stone and magitech chess pieces toward the box, but as soon as he stepped onto the chessboard, a painful electric shock shot through his paws. He sprang back, giving Lunis a warning wave.

The dragon nodded as he slammed a claw into the knight's face, shattering it. "Stay off the board. Got it."

Faraday nodded, diving to the side as a bishop jumped in his direction. He slid between two pawns and kept running, realizing that avoidance was his only method of survival. Lunis took the opposite approach, smashing the attacking pieces. Faraday watched as Plato disappeared inside the glowing box.

He didn't know what kind of magitech could make the lynx powerless, but it had to be incredible. Faraday could only guess what other capabilities the silver box had. He didn't want to find out but believed that before too long, they would. The squirrel had to do what he did best: employ science to help his friends. Faraday ran toward the tower and Kaiser, intent on stopping the madman before it was too late.

CHAPTER TWENTY

"Is that all you've got?" Lunis roared, spitting fire at a pair of pawns. They went up in flames as they tried to close the distance to the blue dragon. Most of the other pieces surrounded Lunis, having moved off the board. "I've defeated a grandmaster in three moves."

He swung around, using his tail to demolish the king. "Yeah, I stood up, picked up a hand, and hit him with it."

Like he was demonstrating this, Lunis swept his claws toward another set of pawns that were guarding the queen. They crumbled on contact.

Lunis had things under control with the chess pieces. That gave Faraday the diversion he needed to sneak into the tower. Kaiser's attention was split between the battle with the dragon and the silver box where Plato was imprisoned.

When he approached the tower, Faraday paused, realizing it was probably guarded like the chessboard. Plato had said it would be shielded from attack. However, Faraday didn't want to assault the tower. Also, he reasoned that if Kaiser was inside it, it wasn't electrified. He hypothesized that whereas attacks would be prevented, a small guest would be permitted if he entered at the right spot.

Now that he was close to the tower, Faraday realized the bottom half was crisscrossed with wires. Glancing up, he saw Kaiser standing next to the rail at the top of the tower, holding the remote in his hand. The mogul had an evil glint in his eyes.

"It's an antenna," Faraday muttered, feeling a rush.

Of course the tower would serve a purpose, Faraday reasoned. It wasn't just a high vantage point from which to watch the chess match. In magitech, everything had a utilitarian purpose, and if the man didn't have magic anymore, he'd need a way to amplify the signal sent from the remote.

"The tower is his transmitter between the remote and the silver contraption," Faraday mumbled, searching for an opening in the bottom of the tower. Someplace that seemed safe to enter and provided a good place to work.

Finding a small opening opposite where Plato was trapped beside the chessboard, Faraday dove into the tower. He held his breath until he was through the wires and hadn't been electrocuted. Relieved, he examined the complex wiring that ran to the top of the tower.

The remote might work near the silver box, but not from a distance, and because of the electrified chessboard, Kaiser had to be far from the device. The magitech box had obviously rendered Plato powerless, transporting him through the air against his will. Faraday was certain that wasn't all the device did, but he knew he'd find out very soon.

Out on the grounds, the sounds of Lunis battling the magitech chess pieces filled the air. However, Faraday kept his focus on disabling the antenna. If he could do that, the remote wouldn't work anymore, and whatever Kaiser had planned would be foiled.

"There, there, little kitty," Kaiser said from above where Faraday was working to sever the wires from the underground power source. "Are you comfortable in your box? I really hope not."

A roar shot through the air, indicating that Lunis was struggling, outnumbered by the chess pieces. Wings beat, followed by a blast of fire. Lunis might be challenged, but Faraday's money was still on the blue dragon.

Like a beaver felling a hundred-year-old oak tree, Faraday chewed through a huge bundle of wires. Sparks shot through the air, but he ducked, the smell of his singed fur filling the air.

"What was that?" Kaiser asked, startled.

"That was me kicking your rook's butt," Lunis replied, covering for Faraday. The sparks and destruction in the tower would have gotten the man's attention, but the dragon was great at distractions. "Here, do you want to check him out for yourself? He made a rookie mistake."

A second later, the broken bits of the demolished rook robot hit the tower, although they didn't harm it, as Faraday had deduced. The tower had a protective shield, but not to keep out trespassers.

"The chess pieces are inconsequential," Kaiser stated. "What I really wanted, I already have."

"Watching me play chess?" Lunis asked as he demolished more pieces.

Faraday had gotten through the main wiring connected to the power source. Only a bit more and the antenna would be dead, which hopefully meant that Plato could be freed.

"You're not playing chess," Kaiser boomed like the blue dragon was serious.

"I don't know how to play chess, but I do know how to put villains in check!"

Faraday couldn't help the chuckle that spilled from his mouth as he sawed through more wires with his sharp teeth.

"Whatever." Kaiser waved dismissively. "What I wanted was to trap Plato, but that's not enough. Today, you deceitful lynx, is your very last. With a press of this final button, your ability to regenerate will be gone. Then just one shot, and you'll be done."

Another chess piece was hurled at the tower to no effect. The tower was still shielded, which meant the power source hadn't been disconnected yet.

"Is that a gun?" Lunis yelled. "You coward, you plan on shooting Plato?"

"Yes, and this time, there won't be any coming back for him," Kaiser answered proudly.

Faraday grabbed the last thick rope of wires in front of him and opened his mouth wide before chomping through them cleanly.

"Say goodbye, Plato," Kaiser roared evilly. "Today, I rid this world of you."

CHAPTER TWENTY-TWO

The humming that had filled the tower disappeared. Faraday hadn't realized it had been filling his ears, given the competing noises. If it was gone, that meant...

He didn't want to get his hopes up, but there was little else he could do at this point besides attack Kaiser by himself. He left the tower and began climbing it from the outside.

However, he was halfway up when a welcome voice came through the air.

"When are you going to learn that you can't win against me?" Plato asked, his voice echoing around them like he was on a loudspeaker.

Faraday glanced over his shoulder to see the lynx sitting smugly on the tile in front of the silver box, free.

When the power source was disconnected, it had disabled the electricity in the chessboard. It also appeared to have deactivated the remote, freeing Plato and thankfully turning off the magitech that would prevent regeneration if he was shot.

"What! How? Oh, I've had enough of you, cat!" Kaiser yelled frantically.

A *click* echoed—the sound of a gun being cocked. Faraday

sped up, racing to the top. If he got up there quickly, he could attack Kaiser from behind and get the gun away from him.

"If you shoot me, I'll just come back," Plato stated with confidence.

Kaiser laughed. "Yes, but if I shoot the queen, the bombs all over the city will detonate. I knew you'd bring your friends to help and that the blue dragon would fight my chess pieces. And win-win for me when he destroyed the queen, the trigger for the bombs. Then you'd know it was you who had killed so many in Tortugas Locas."

Still climbing furiously, Faraday chanced a glance over his shoulder. He caught sight of Lunis standing between the bishops, a knight, and a rook. Behind them was the queen they'd been guarding. They were in a standoff.

Faraday spilled over the edge of the tower and saw Kaiser point the gun at the white queen, a triumphant look on his face. The squirrel was about to attack Kaiser from behind when Plato spoke, making everyone pause.

"It's unfortunate that it's come down to this." His voice was a whisper.

"It really is," Kaiser stated. "Say goodbye to your precious Tortugas Locas. If I can't have your death, I'll take your grief."

"Not today," Plato replied. "You've given me no choice but to end things once and for all. Before, I allowed you to live."

"You stripped me of my powers and imprisoned me!" Kaiser snapped, his body shaking. Faraday was prepared to jump, but something in Plato's gaze told him not to—a brief look he'd shot him while Kaiser was ranting.

"I punished you for your crimes," Plato said simply. "But now, I'm forced to rid this world of you. It's clear you can't be rehabilitated."

"Rid this world of me?" Kaiser laughed like that was funny. "I'm about to detonate a hundred bombs all over this city. Say goodbye to this place."

"Goodbye…to you, Kaiser." Plato smiled.

There was a loud *bang*, and a huge puff of smoke rose where Kaiser had been standing. The gun clattered to the floor.

Faraday blinked to make sense of what he'd just seen. Kaiser had simply disappeared. Aside from the gun, there was no sign of the man.

Lunis had stopped fighting the chess pieces, which had lost power along with the tower.

Plato stood in the middle of the chessboard with a look of great wisdom and weight on his face. A spark flew from the lynx's eyes, and Faraday knew that he did what he had to do. In a show of power, Plato had removed Kaiser from this planet. It was obviously not something he liked to do or would abuse, but the lynx had been given great power because he was pure and used it for only good.

CHAPTER TWENTY-THREE

"Using your power in front of us... Did that..." Faraday began as they stared at the aquamarine water.

"It cost me a life," Plato answered matter-of-factly. "But only one."

"Man, you can just make someone not exist anymore with a blink of your eye," Lunis gushed, kicking up sand on the beach like he was going to make a sandcastle.

"It requires a bit more than that," Plato argued. "I have to twitch my tail, too."

Faraday and Lunis snickered.

"Well, after this, I never want to play chess again," Lunis related, looking up as three figures approached from down the beach. The wind was tangling their hair, and their clothes suggested they'd just returned from a battle.

The Beaufont women were always beautiful, but especially after battles when their faces were flushed, their blonde hair was askew, and their eyes were filled with determination and triumph.

"I didn't realize you played a lot of chess," Faraday said, his heart beating fast at the sight of Paris striding next to her mother and aunt. It had only been three days, but he had missed his sidekick.

"Oh, I don't play," Lunis answered. "Not since I had lunch with that chess master. It was at a diner with checkered tablecloths. It took her three hours to pass me the salt."

Faraday was surprised at the chuckle that fell out of Plato's mouth. "Good one, Lun."

"Thanks, Play," the dragon retorted as Liv, Sophia, and Paris halted in front of their familiars, who were lounging on the beach, soaking up the Mexican sun.

"Hey, you big lazy loaf," Sophia started, toeing her dragon's tail, which was curled up around him. "You appear to be enjoying your relaxing vacation."

"It wasn't really all that relaxing," Lunis muttered, giving her a look of adoration.

Liv swept her arm at the shimmering blue ocean. "Yeah, this looks very stressful."

"Appearances can be deceiving," Plato muttered dryly.

"Yeah, that's true coming from you, little kitty," Liv stated. "Have you secretly saved the world while pretending to take catnaps?"

He blinked at her. "You know me so well."

"That I do," she agreed.

"Well, I don't know about you guys," Paris interjected, stretching her arms over her head. "But I've had a long three days and could really use some R and R. If you aren't bored with lounging on the beach, maybe we can stay for a few more days to unwind."

Faraday glanced at Lunis and Plato, and the three exchanged knowing looks. "I think we can extend our vacation a few more days, but only three."

"That does seem to be the magic number." Plato's wise old eyes glinted. "The best things in life come in threes."

The three Beaufonts and their three magical friends took the next three days to enjoy a much-deserved vacation.

For the time being, the world was safe. When it needed a hero, a Beaufont and her familiar would be there to save the day once again.

SARAH'S AUTHOR NOTES

WRITTEN DECEMBER 14, 2021

A huge thank you to all of you for reading our books, these short stories and putting up with my author notes. Thank you to all of the readers and the LMBPN team.

Unlike Bird Killer, I don't shoot BBs at woodland creatures.

Still regret telling me that story, huh, Mike?

So when I was a child, I didn't play with BB guns. I simply frolicked around the woods and lake where I lived in East Texas. One day, while rambling onto myself about a story in my head, I realized that a squirrel was sort of stalking me. So I picked a pecan from the tree in our yard, broke it open and offered a nut to the squirrel.

Moments later and I literally had a squirrel eating out of my hand. My mom, who had taken a break from watching her soap operas and was checking to see that I was still alive, glanced out the window from our house. When she found me with a possibly rabid rodent taking things from my hand, she ran for the yard, screaming.

I explained to the irate woman that the squirrel was friendly and that I'd named him Sammy. Although reluctant, my mother couldn't discount the fact that Sammy wasn't posing any threat to me. Actually he was following me around the yard, curious about what I was up to and seemingly wanting to be involved.

Later, Sammy became known for strolling on into the house when we left the door open. I'd find him eating fruit on the dining room table or rummaging through grocery bags in the kitchen. If I was out in the yard then the little squirrel would often join me, curious about my adventures around the lake.

And that's where the influence of Faraday came from. Also squirrels are cute and have a lot of personality.

I often enjoy watching them cackle at my cats, taunting them from the trees. Of course, it's not so cute when the little jerks steal the unripen oranges from my tree, take a bite, realize it's not ready yet and throw it down on the patio to rot. Then the tiny-brained rodents do it again the next day.

At least Faraday is a smart squirrel. I loved the idea of an unsuspecting nerdy squirrel. It goes in line with the other familiars who all are not as they'd seem. A dragon who cracks jokes and a cat who is knows everything aren't what we'd expect, which makes it all the more fun.

I loved writing these short stories more than I would have imagined. It was fun weaving them all together. And the way it ended with the symbolism of three was unexpected. But then I was like, of course the magic number had to be three. Three Beaufonts. Three animals. Three days.

Soon I'll return to Paris' next series, but the break has been nice. And writing this story reminded me of how much I love that scientific squirrel. Just keep Bird Killer away from him with his BB gun. You're welcome, Mike.

Much love and Peace,
Tiny Ninja

MICHAEL'S AUTHOR NOTES

WRITTEN JANUARY 13, 2022

Thank you for not only reading this series but these author notes here in the back as well.

Sarah mentions going to Scotland for castles and dragons (and LURRRVVVVEEE), which is funny as hell because the Sarah I originally met was not "that" girl who would fall head-over-heels in love with any guy.

She was too headstrong, and that just wasn't her. If you don't believe me, go pick up a copy (or listen to the audio) of *Everyone in LA is an Asshole* by Sarah Fuller. Fuller (I am thinking) was her pseudonym for "Full of Shit."

At least she kept the same first name, *#amIright*? Otherwise, not sure if she was going to be able to keep which author name she was responding to correct. BWAHAHAHAHA… She's going to diss me again; I just know it.

In fact, I'll drop the blurb here, and let's see if YOU can pick out the Sarah "Fuller" in this:

LA is a beast. A city that swallows most with its glamour and glitz.

Not Sarah Fuller, though.

Stubborn and relentless, Sarah refuses to be changed by her surroundings. Often, she takes a cynical approach, judging the world around her, though never taking anything too seriously.

Thrown back into the dating arena in her late thirties, Sarah encounters brand new challenges.

Readers will laugh out loud at the adventures and mishaps this sassy protagonist gets herself into. She explores LA life, seeing it through her unique lens.

Hair extensions, goat yoga, socialites and all the strangeness that comes out of LA weave together in this crazy, episodic adventure.

Can you handle the absurdities?

Scroll back up and hit the 'Read Now' or 'Buy' button and laugh until you can't see.

Fans of Chelsea Handler and Sex in the City will love Everyone in LA is an Asshole, *a series that doesn't hold back and says what we're all secretly thinking.*

I'll drop the link to the book on Amazon here for those who really want to know what goes on in Sarah's brain. At least, Sarah's brain in her 2018. I tell you, falling in love really threw a wrench into her sarcastic dating life.

Everyone in LA is an Asshole (Amazon link)

As her publisher, I am just letting everyone know and attempting to bring more attention so she earns some more money on the book. I am in no way, shape, or form pointing out how right I am about pre-boyfriend Sarah Fuller and post-boyfriend Sarah Noffke.

;-)

Have a great week or weekend, and talk to you in the next story!

Ad Aeternitatem,

Michael Anderle

ACKNOWLEDGMENTS

SARAH NOFFKE

Thank you to the readers, the awesome people at LMBP and to my friends and family. For this story, I owe a special thank you to my cat, Finley. He is the direct inspiration for Plato. The cover designer actually used a picture of him for this book and it's spot on. Finley is so lovable and loving and one of my best friends. And I like to think his sage wisdom comes through in subtle ways, just like Plato. However, he has no magic, that I know of.

I have so many people to thank who make writing these books and stories possible. I feel so grateful to have so many awesome supporters. My daughter is my muse and she puts up with my eccentric ways. And my friends, although they don't always want to know the details of the stories I'm writing, are very supportive.

But you all, the readers, really make this all possible. Thank you! I hope you continue to enjoy the stories because I have no plans of quitting.

Love,
Tiny Ninja

CONNECT WITH THE AUTHORS

Connect with Sarah and sign up for her email list here:

http://www.sarahnoffke.com/connect/

Michael Anderle Social

Website: http://lmbpn.com

Email List: http://lmbpn.com/email/

https://www.facebook.com/LMBPNPublishing

https://twitter.com/MichaelAnderle

https://www.instagram.com/lmbpn_publishing/

https://www.bookbub.com/authors/michael-anderle